'I don't argue all the time,' Melanie said quickly.

Then she chuckled, caught out in doing what she denied. Looking across at his face, she was shocked by the deep lines of strain or tiredness beneath its blankness.

'Well, not normally,' she added lightly, to cover her dismay. 'Maybe it's a reversion to teenage habits caused by the shock of seeing you again after all these years.'

'The past coming back to haunt you, Melly?' Peter asked.

Dear Reader

We look at special care baby units with Josie Metcalfe's SECRETS TO KEEP, Caroline Anderson returns to the obstetrics unit—more babies—at the Audley Memorial in ANYONE CAN DREAM, while each heroine has a secret to keep from the hero. You will *love* William and Jacob!

We welcome back Sharon Wirdnam with CASUALTY OF PASSION, Meredith Webber's UNRULY HEART repatriates ill people and both books bring couples back together. A good month's reading!

The Editor

Having pursued many careers—from schoolteaching to pig farming—with varying degrees of success and plenty of enjoyment, **Meredith Webber** seized on the arrival of a computer in her house as an excuse to turn to what had always been a secret urge—writing. As she had more doctors and nurses in the family than any other professional people, the medical romance seemed the way to go! Meredith lives on the Gold Coast of Queensland, with her husband and teenage son.

Recent titles by the same author:

A DIFFERENT DESTINY
WHISPER IN THE HEART
A TESTING TIME

UNRULY
HEART

BY
MEREDITH WEBBER

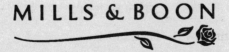

MILLS & BOON

MILLS & BOON LIMITED
ETON HOUSE, 18–24 PARADISE ROAD
RICHMOND, SURREY, TW9 1SR

First published in Great Britain 1995
by Mills & Boon Limited

© Meredith Webber 1995

Australian copyright 1995   Philippine copyright 1995
This edition 1995

ISBN 0 263 78971 3

Set in 10 on 12 pt Linotron Times
03-9502-53169

Typeset in Great Britain by Centracet, Cambridge
Made and printed in Great Britain

CHAPTER ONE

MELANIE listened with something approaching awe as Jan Stevens gave brief outlines of some of the repatriation cases UniversAid had handled. The strange tingling sensation flooding through her body told her how much she wanted the job, but outwardly she remained composed, her excitement only visible as an extra gleam in her soft brown eyes, and a straining whiteness in her tensely clasped hands.

'We need people with common sense,' Jan continued. 'Cool, unflappable operators who will be able to handle frightened people shrieking abuse at them in a foreign language from half a world away.'

'I can understand that,' Melanie assured her. 'I've had some experience in unusual situations and I know that staying calm and thinking rationally is the safest course to take.'

Jan nodded, rifling through the pages of Melanie's application and rereading the page that Melanie knew was a reference from her field manager during her work as a volunteer in Botswana.

'Yes,' Jan confirmed at last. 'With your language skills and broad nursing experience, I do think you're the person we've been looking for, although——'

Melanie held her breath. Could there be some computer link-up between medical repatriation services? Would a case from eight years ago make lights flash against her name when it was typed into the data base? She could feel tiny beads of perspiration forming

around her hairline, and unclenched her fingers to raise
one hand and push the thick blonde hair back from her
forehead.

'—you're younger than most of our nursing staff. In
the past, we have tried to employ more mature
women.'

'I'm twenty-six,' Melanie objected, sighing with
relief yet fearful that she might now lose this fantastic
opportunity because of her age.

Jan smiled.

'I was talking forty-plus maturity,' she said wryly,
shuffling the papers back into a neat pile, 'but no one
in that age range who can speak Spanish and French
has applied, and the fact that you can throw in
Portuguese and a bit of Shona dialect is an added
bonus. With the trekking companies moving into
Africa and many young people working as volunteers
over there, we are operating in Africa more often than
we have previously. For the same reason, the South
American business is also increasing.'

Was that a definite maybe? Melanie wondered,
aware that she was finding it hard to breathe as she
waited for Jan's decision.

'You do understand that this full-time position
entails long, boring hours on the telephone. Some of
our part-time staff work specific shifts, some do only
telephone work, while our doctors and a few of our
nursing staff are only on call for emergencies and
repatriation trips. In this position, you'll be involved in
every aspect of UniversAid, not just a constant round
of world travel at company expense, a dozen missions
of mercy in a month!'

Did this mean she had the job?

She responded quickly. 'Of course I realise that. I

imagine being able to provide immediate reassurance to people by phone would prove as rewarding as physically bringing them home. I believe the work UniversAid does is so necessary, so important to people in trouble anywhere in the world, that being even a small cog in the wheel would be rewarding.'

'I happen to agree with you,' Jan told her, a warm smile now lighting her eyes and transforming her placid face to one of glowing attractiveness. 'I also happen to think you'll make an excellent employee.'

The excitement became an excited, bubbling joy, and Melanie felt her face split by a huge, delighted grin that nothing Jan still had to say could totally erase.

'There is, of course, a two-month trial period during which time you can see if you like working for us, as well as our being able to gauge your suitability. You'll start by sitting in with one of our phone operators in the command-room, then progress to taking calls on the morning shift, which is the least hectic.'

Again, Melanie nodded, and her smile faded. Initial elation was turning to trepidation as she realised the responsibility that would be placed on her, taking calls from travellers in trouble, often in remote parts of the world, and organising help and support for them.

Then Jan was speaking again, and she forced the concern away and concentrated on what the administrator was telling her.

'In a few weeks, you'll do a stint of night duty, to make sure you can handle the isolation and function well with fewer supports. By the time your trial period is over, you should have a good idea of the scope of our work, and we'll have a good idea of your ability to cope. Any questions?'

'Only one,' Melanie said, nervous laughter making the words tremble slightly. 'When do I start?'

'Nine o'clock, Monday,' Jan replied. 'Now, if you've the time, I'll show you around and introduce you to the staff on duty.'

Rising to her feet to follow Jan from the neat office, Melanie resisted an almost overwhelming urge to skip and dance in sheer joyous relief. She had been granted this trial because she had shown herself sensible, mature, calm and efficient, which meant that any physical demonstration of her delight would have to wait until she was well away from the offices of UniversAid.

Jan led the way past empty glass-walled offices, explaining as she went, 'It rarely gets busy before eleven, so our airline specialist, Bill Gates, doesn't start work till ten. He makes all bookings, charters planes where necessary, and can tell you who to see in Bogata, for instance, if you need a plane that can land on a short strip, at altitude, but still hold a stretcher.'

Melanie shook her head in wonder at such encyclo-paedic knowledge, then realised that the man was as much a specialist as any doctor or nurse who pursued further training in a particular field.

'The next office is that of our medical director. He may be in before you leave. He's supposed to be off duty after bringing back a heart attack patient from Riga yesterday, but UniversAid is his baby and I think it would take surgical intervention to remove him from it for long.'

'If he feels that way, he's probably better off here than pretending to relax at his home,' Melanie responded, picking up a faint thread of expectation—

or was it challenge?—in the air that made her sympathetic to the absent man's actions.

'And this is the heart of UniversAid,' Jan announced, throwing open the door to a wide, bright room. In front of the windows, two banks of desks faced a wide, curving wall that held whiteboards divided into columns, a huge map of the world, and flashing digital clocks announcing the time in New York, Los Angeles, Tokyo, Moscow, Athens, Paris and London.

Phones rang, computers hummed, and the operators' quiet voices murmured instructions and advice. The whole effect was of an orchestrated efficiency that made Melanie shake her head in wonder.

'The back row of phones deals mainly with domestic and vehicle insurance and car problems, as we provide a twenty-four-hour assist service for corporate clients. The front row is travel, with many of our callers seeking advice about medical precautions to take prior to setting out. "Should I have a smallpox vaccination?" is still the most common.'

'Because people won't believe their doctors that smallpox has been completely wiped out?' Melanie asked.

'Precisely!' Jan told her, introducing her to the room at large and naming the staff who were present, before turning back towards the door. 'I suppose I can understand it,' she added. 'It was a decade before health authorities who oversaw the massive vaccination programme could bring themselves to believe that they hadn't missed a tiny village somewhere in the world, where the scourge still lingered!'

They moved out into the passage and Melanie turned to pull the door of the operations-room closed.

'Ah, Peter has arrived,' Jan announced happily.
'Come in and I'll introduce you.'

Responding to a tugging hand on her arm, Melanie
turned, her eyes caught by the movement behind the
glass partition. Then her heart stopped beating.

It was impossible! It couldn't possibly be! Not after
all this time! Not here in Brisbane, of all places!

'Come on,' Jan was saying, dragging at her arm, but
her mind whirled in such chaos that she was unable to
order her feet to move.

'You're not shy, are you?'

She could hear laughter, but also a faint edge of
doubt in Jan's voice. A shy courier would be useless!

One foot moved forward, and the other followed,
mechanical movements made through a thick fog of
despair. They wouldn't need a computer to check on
her, not when they had the man whose report would
have provided the original details of her medical repatriation from Portugal.

'This is Melanie Ashcroft, Peter. Melanie, this is
Peter Wade, our founder, medical director, and rescuer
extraordinaire!'

There was a note of almost possessive pride in the
introduction that lanced through Melanie's confusion.
Yet for a moment she still hesitated, her gaze flickering
quickly over the thin, dark face of the man on his feet
behind the wide cedar desk.

'I've met Dr Wade,' she mumbled through lips stiff
with the realisation that he did remember her.

This dream job, so nearly hers, was not going to be
saved by any lapse of his memory! Her one brief
glimpse of dark eyebrows almost meeting above his
long-lashed eyes, pinched nostrils and a thin slash of

lips had told her that the anger she had provoked eight years ago was something else he hadn't forgotten.

'How are you, Melanie?' he asked formally, the melodious English voice overlaid with an austere politeness.

Berfore she could find the words for a meaningless response, Jan said quickly, 'I wonder if you'd mind waiting in my office for a moment, Melanie? There are a few messages I have to pass on to Peter, then I'll take you down in the lift.'

So even practical, sensible Jan had picked up on the explosive, atmospheric disturbance that her meeting with the boss had caused, Melanie realised as she hurried thankfully back to the sanctuary of Jan's panelled room. Would they conjure up some reason why Jan's decision was to be set aside, or would she simply be told she was unsuitable?

She sank into the comfortable chair beside the desk, her mind battling against memories she'd thought were buried forever. With grim determination, she forced them back, breathing deeply to regain her physical balance and settle her erratic pulse.

The distorted voices had been mere background noise, until she finally relaxed into the chair, the past under control and the present almost ready for review.

There are other jobs, she was assuring herself, when the sounds became words—words that she was not meant to be hearing.

'I tell you she was out of control,' the clipped voice was saying. 'A wild raver who'd run away from her host family and taken up with a bunch of kids who made your hair curl even to look at them.'

There was an inaudible rejoinder, then the deeper voice continued, 'She wasn't the first exchange student

I repatriated for Worldwide, Jan. I'd seen some pretty pathetic sights, but nothing approaching the behaviour of that young madam.'

Shrinking back into the chair, Melanie raised her hands to her ears, meaning to shut out the man's scorn and anger, but curiosity—or was it an instinct for self-preservation?—made her pause, and lean forward to try to pick up what the administrator was saying.

'——best qualified, in fact the only person who applied who actually met all the criteria—which you set yourself.'

There was a dark muttering noise, overlaid by Jan's calm reasoning. 'Support staff are my responsibility,' she was pointing out, 'and, after all, it's eight years since the girl was in trouble, and her references and recommendations are proof that she's got her act together since then.'

Melanie stood up and took a step towards the desk, trying to track down the source of the conversation. Hearing Jan's defence filled her with a guilty unease, and she studied the complicated phone, assuming it must have a conference function that was activated at the moment, making it an effective intercom. Her fingers hovered indecisively over the buttons.

It was patently obvious that Peter Wade was far from happy, although his next words were unclear. Had he walked away from the desk and turned his back to Jan as he voiced more objections? Were his fingers clenched into a white-knuckled fury as they had been with her once before?

'Well, I've already told her she's got the job,' Jan interrupted abruptly, 'but I did explain about the two-month trial. If you're convinced of her unsuitability we needn't keep her on, and, in the meantime, you don't have to have anything to do with her.'

The words had a finality that sent Melanie scuttling back to her seat. With any luck, Dr Wade would stay in his office and sulk for a while, and Jan would not realise that their conversation had been broadcast.

The excitement she had felt earlier vanished like mist beneath the rising sun and it was a strain to find a smile to hide her disappointment.

'Sorry to keep you waiting,' Jan said briskly. 'With people coming and going all the time, we have to grab any opportunity to pass on information.'

Melanie watched warily while the older woman reached for a set of keys on the neat desk. Surely Jan would want to know details of the long-past escapade!

'Come on, I'll take you down in the lift. I'm afraid all the security seems paranoid to new staff and visitors, but with the mass of data on our computers it's essential.'

She led the way back to the lift, summoned it, then activated its return to the ground floor with a special key that slid into a slot low down on the control panel. Melanie's stomach clenched into a tight knot as she waited for the questions that would probably end her career at UniversAid before it began.

'When you come in on Monday, go up to Reception on level one, and someone will go down and work the lift for you to access the control-room floor. This is standard practice for all our new employees while they are on trial, from the best qualified doctors down to the janitorial staff. You'll get used to it.'

'It does seem extreme, but I had assumed it was to protect staff on night duty.' Melanie struggled to sound as if nothing had happened to disturb her.

'That too,' Jan agreed. 'But data security is paramount. We can access the fourth-floor offices with our plates, but the fifth floor, where the computers are kept, is off-limits to everyone but our computer programmer and Peter. Once you're into the swing of things, you'll usually find someone working your shift will be coming in at the same time, and you'll come up with them.'

The lift came to a silent halt as Melanie ran through the words in her mind, trying to make sense of a reprieve she could barely believe. Jan ushered her out with a warm smile that effectively hid any consternation she might be feeling about her boss's disclosures.

'See you Monday, Melanie,' she said as the doors closed, and Melanie was left in the foyer, wondering if the words were a threat or a promise.

'It's a power struggle between the two of them,' her friend Kip announced a little later as they sat over coffee in a pavement café around the corner from the UniversAid offices.

She had listened in silence to Melanie's recital, and, after two fresh Danish pastries, had finally found a satisfactory solution to the question of why Melanie was still to be employed. 'She's in charge of the appointments and that's that! Maybe he's been throwing his weight around in her section for too long, and she's determined to put him back in his place.'

'But if he's the founder of the service, then he probably owns the entire business, which kills your power struggle theory.' Melanie squinted as sunlight from a passing car threw a dazzle of light into her eyes. 'Besides, he's not a "throwing weight around" kind of person—or he wasn't eight years ago.'

'I thought you told me he'd dragged you kicking and screaming back home——real caveman stuff!' Kip complained. 'I've always put your hang-up about the man—all men in fact—down to the fact that it was physically confrontational—something you'd never experienced before in your family of gentle, refined academics.'

She sounded so aggrieved that Melanie had to smile, in spite of the dismay still seeping through her. Long before Kip had obtained her major in psychology, she had constantly analysed her friends' behaviour, changing her theories with blithe good humour, and ignoring the often glaring inconsistencies in her arguments.

'Sorry, Kip,' she said, a slight smile playing about her lips as she fixed her eyes firmly on her friend's face. 'Peter Wade is *the* most civilised man I have ever met, and while I'm in denial mode I'd like to point out that I *do not* have a hang-up about him or men in general. I simply prefer the single state and an uncomplicated life. I'm a travel freak, remember!' she added with a laugh.

'As if I hadn't noticed!'

Smiling at the resignation in Kip's voice, Melanie pushed the plate containing the remaining pastry towards her friend, before adding, 'Not that any of this raking through my past or discussion of the present is helpful. It's the future I'm concerned about—specifically Monday, and the beginning of my "trial" at UniversAid.'

Kip looked perplexed, her blue eyes peering across the table at Melanie as if she hoped to read her unspoken thoughts.

'Do you want the job, Mel?' she asked, and Melanie looked away from her puzzled scrutiny, staring out across the traffic that filtered slowly past them in a steady stream.

'Of course I do!' she replied. 'It's like an answer to all my dreams—to be able to combine work and travel. And it's an opportunity to do more than ward nursing, to pit my ability and ingenuity against a different set of circumstances every moment of the day, and find solutions. It's a challenge, Kip!'

Hearing the ardent enthusiasm in her own voice, she shook her head, trying to regain the composure that had helped her through her interview. Drawing a steadying breath, she added, 'But if I'm not going to be officially appointed in two months' time, is it worth starting? I don't know if I can cope with learning the ins and outs of it, and making new friends—not to mention the inoculations!—knowing all the time I won't be appointed to the permanent staff.'

'You can't be sure of that,' Kip asserted, slapping a hand down on the table with such force that the coffee-cups rattled. 'OK, so you're on trial, but unless you're hopeless at the work, or blow all their computer fuses, they can't really put you off.'

'Even if the boss doesn't want me working there? Come on, my friend, let's have some realism here!' Melanie picked up a teaspoon from her saucer and twisted it in her fingers, watching the futile movement to avoid her friend's perceptive eyes. Would Kip hear the quiver of despair in her voice?

'Well, I don't think they can,' Kip said stoutly. 'It will be up to you to make certain that you're the best damn apprentice they ever had—then they can't possibly let you go. What's more, you've always said you'd like a chance to have that part of your life over again.'

There was a silence that dragged on until Melanie

was forced to look up at her. She found her eyes caught, and held, by her friend's stern gaze.

'Well, this is it, handed to you on a plate. This is the perfect opportunity to prove to that man, who totally misjudged you at the time, from the little you've told me——' there was a meaningful pause that Melanie ignored; she'd kept her own counsel for eight years, and was hardly about to pour out all the humiliation and pain of that period now '—that you are an extremely competent, capable, caring and utterly worthwhile human being, beside being my best friend!'

She pushed back her chair as she finished this accolade, and came around the table to drop an arm round Melanie's shoulders and give her a quick hug.

'I've got to get back to work so I'll see you tonight. Go out and buy yourself something. That never fails to cheer me up!'

Melanie watched her friend's well-dressed figure wend its way through the tables, and sighed as she disappeared from sight. Advice always sounded simple when it was spoken but she was well aware that the reality was never as easy.

An icy shiver shook her frame as the ghost of the past rattled up her backbone, and filled her with a cold dread. Could Kip be right? Would contact with the man who had witnessed her mad belligerence lay the spectre of her time in Portugal forever? Had some particularly malignant fate produced this twist in her life as a test of some description? And if fates existed, what benighted spirit had made that stiff and proper English gentleman, Dr Peter Wade, desert his native land and start his business on the other side of the world in subtropical Brisbane?

'May I join you?'

The blood froze in her veins. She did not need to lift her head to know who had spoken, so she focused on the bit of dark suit in her field of vision and nodded mutely.

Here's your chance to find the answer to at least one question, a small imp of self-preservation whispered in her head as she heard the deep, English-accented voice again.

'I won't bite you, Melly!'

The words brought her head jerking up and the old retort, 'Don't call me Melly,' flew off her tongue before conscious thought could prevent it.

His eyes, a clear pale blue that reminded her of skies above deserted places, were fixed on her face, and his expression was unreadable behind the stillness of his face.

Had Kip been right? she wondered as her body reacted to his scrutiny with a wayward lurch of her heart and a skittering rush of blood through her veins. Peter Wade might not have used physical force on her, but there had been a physical element to their struggle, on her side anyway.

The blush started at her toes and worked its way up, burning through her body in an enveloping tidal wave of shame, as that one fleeting thought liberated another shred of memory she had completely blanked out until this moment.

'If you're the boss, I'd rather you sack me now than give me two months of a pretend trial,' she blurted out, as much to hide her embarrassment as for any rational reason.

He lowered his head, as if conceding her right to the tetchy statement, then turned to thank the waitress who had placed a cup of coffee on the table in front of him. His beautiful manners had shamed her once before!

Melanie watched his hand reach out, and his thin, bony fingers spoon sugar into the black brew, while the silence grew and grew.

'Jan showed me your application. I can't fault her selection based on your experience and qualifications,' he said eventually, his eyes lifting to meet hers, his face still expressionless.

A large 'but' seemed to hover in the air between them, and Melanie turned away, her heart hammering crazily in her chest. Was she 'hung-up' over this man, as Kip had suggested, or was her reaction to him all mixed up with the turbulent shame and horror of that bit of her past? He was speaking again, and she concentrated on the words to blot out the memories that his reappearance in her life had unleashed.

'It seems that once you settled back down at home you worked hard at becoming a responsible adult. If that's the case, I'll be happy to have you on the staff.'

A hint of doubt still shadowed the words, making them sound more like a reproach than a compliment, and Melanie felt a tiny spurt of anger, sharp and hot, stab through her, but she bit back a sniping retort, then wondered if he was deliberately testing her composure with his subtle provocation.

With a considerable effort she forced herself to act as the calm, composed applicant who had impressed Jan Stevens. A question usually solved a social hiatus, and besides, beyond her shock at finding him here, she was curious.

'What made you choose Brisbane to set up in opposition to Worldwide?'

'I set up in Australia so I wouldn't be in opposition,'

he told her, his eyes meeting hers over the rim of his raised coffee-cup. 'There was no medical repatriation service here when I started, and it fitted in with a loose network of affiliates Worldwide was gathering up, to provide on-the-spot support without too much expensive infrastructure or outlays on their part.'

A wintry smile plucked the corners of his mouth upwards as he added, 'I spent a few days in Brisbane once, after delivering a patient to a town not far south of here. It was the only city in Australia I knew!'

Her eyes had caught that flicker of movement and were held by the shapely lips, no longer thinned in disapproval. Irrationally, she wanted to see the smile widen, but the reference was too obvious a lure and she skipped hurriedly past it with another question.

'And what did Cynthia think when you dragged her halfway round the world to this remote outpost of civilisation?' Her mind had dredged up a vivid picture of the elegant brunette who had clung like a limpet to his side while they'd waited at the airport in London for their flight to Australia.

She saw those shapely lips tighten again and her eyes swept up, but his head was turning towards the traffic, and any expression that might have flickered in his eyes was hidden from her.

'Cynthia had very little to say,' he said quietly. 'She realised early in our courtship that the logistics of a job like this make even the most casual of arrangements difficult. The unpredictability is a great strain on relationships, as Jan has, no doubt, pointed out to you.'

'With so many people working in this business and other jobs that require frequent absences from home, there must be plenty who can maintain successful relationships in spite of the irregularity of their work patterns.' Melanie argued automatically, to hide a flicker of inexplicable pain, although relationships were something she avoided assiduously.

Study and work were both enjoyable and satisfying, and the opportunity to work in Africa had fired her with a determination to see as much of the world as she possible could—an ambition that seemed far more realistic and achievable than other young women's dreams of marriage and living happily ever after!

'Maybe the people who wrote such glowing references for you liked a pert little chit who argued with everything they said!'

It took her a few seconds to register the sniping words, as she'd been lost in her own stray thoughts.

'I don't argue all the time,' she said quickly, then chuckled, caught out in doing what she denied. Looking across at his face in the hope of seeing an answering glimmer of laughter, she was shocked by the deep lines of strain or tiredness beneath its blankness.

'Well, not normally,' she added lightly, to cover her dismay. 'Maybe it's a reversion to teenage habits caused by the shock of seeing you again after all these years.'

'The past coming back to haunt you, Melly?' he asked, his voice soft and so low, it sounded curiously husky. And now he smiled, but it wasn't the warm, spontaneous grin that lit up his craggy face, the smile she remembered vividly from the rare occasions she'd seen it. This was more a twisted puckering of the lips, with a hint of world-weary cynicism thrown in, and it shocked Melanie more than his sudden reappearance in her life had done.

'Did you recover completely from the hepatitis—no

recurrences or after-effects?' It was his turn to fill the silence with the cool politeness of a question!

'Completely,' she assured him. 'I had regular SGOT and bilirubin tests for years afterwards, and had the Hep B vaccine when I began nursing.'

'And obviously you've conquered the anorexia.'

She could almost feel his eyes on her lightly tanned skin as they took in the soft contours of her arms, and lingered on the fullness of her breasts.

'It wasn't a clinical case of anorexia nervosa, you know,' she told him carefully, her eyes fixed on his face as she put the facts to him in spite of his earlier comment about her arguing. 'It was a side-effect of the hepatitis! I may have been stupid, but I wasn't silly enough to punish my body deliberately.

'No?' he tempted softly, and again she felt the burning shame, and dropped her head to hide the wash of colour that would betray her.

'I've got to get back to the office,' he said abruptly, rising to his feet. 'Good luck on Monday!'

Then he was striding away, his tall figure erect, neatly suited—the essential businessman. He didn't sound as if he'd meant it when he'd said good luck!

She watched with an unfamiliar feeling of regret, as if she had lost something very precious.

Eight years ago, there'd been a brave and spirited adventurer beneath the façade of the proper English doctor, an intrepid man who loved the challenges presented by distance and medical emergencies, and who conquered them with all the determined zeal of an old-world explorer.

She'd fought him every inch of the way home, kicking and spitting as viciously as a trapped cat attacking a rescuer. He'd found her in the basic clinic at Monsanto where she'd drifted with a gang of 'no-hopers', as he'd called them, and somehow chivvied and coaxed her back to her home on the Gold Coast, an hour's drive south of Brisbane. Once home, he'd handed her back to her parents with a list of medical instructions and some harsh words about their methods of child-raising.

Poor loves! As if any of it had been their fault.

And what of Peter Wade? Did the adventurer still lurk beneath that civilised exterior, or had the cynicism she now recognised in him swept away the inexplicable joy and wonder of reaching new frontiers and finding a way through unfamiliar territory?

CHAPTER TWO

ONE month of handling the telephone calls and computer data had given Melanie a confidence that prompted excitement rather than trepidation as she rode up in the lift with Rose, her co-worker on this, her first night shift. It was only eight o'clock, but the lamplit streets, the absence of traffic noise, and the hushed, dark building added to a feeling of adventure.

There was little time to savour the moment! The phone demanded attention as she settled into the chair, the caller a doctor from West Australia puzzled over a patient recently returned from China who was now suffering a high fever.

'I've ruled out malaria, which was unlikely anyway, and the salmonella viruses. He was in good health for a couple of weeks after his return, but is now suffering severe abdominal pain as well as the fever.'

While the man detailed his patient's symptoms, Melanie's fingers brought China up on the computer screen and her eyes scanned the rolling lines of information. As different districts offered their own peculiar health hazards, she opened the atlas on her desk to a map of China and asked, 'Where exactly was he?'

'Just a minute, I'll check his file,' came the quick reply, and her fingers hit the 'pause' button to hold the district menu in place.

'He was white-water kayaking in a place called Tiger's Leap Gorge on the Yangtze.'

The information quacked into her ear, and she

sighed. That was a great help! Even with her elementary knowledge of China, she was aware that the Yangtze was one of the longest rivers in the world—it would cross many districts, and pass through two or three different climatic zones.

'Could you hold for a moment?' she said, and concentrated on the map.

Finding the Yangtze, she followed it up towards its source, knowing that the gorge was unlikely to be marked on such an elementary map. Beside her Rose was speaking quietly, and she was vaguely aware that someone else had entered the room, but her mind was on the pale contour lines, working out that a gorge would run through mountains and have steep sides. This meant it should have closer contour marks.

Sichuan Province had mountains and a mass of wiggly lines near the river. She brought it up on the screen, but it offered nothing. Should she persevere with the area or go to arthropod-borne diseases in another file and start from there?

Then her mind seized its own faint clue, following it as swiftly as any computer. Kayaking—water—schistosomiasis—bilharziasis, borne by a little worm that lived in fresh water. Surely this far up the Yangtze would be fresh!

'Have you thought of bilharziasis?' she asked the patient man at the other end of the line as excitement coursed through her. It was like a game, this chase through electronic files to find an elusive clue!

She concentrated now on the screen, delving deeper and deeper into the computer's massive data banks until Schistosoma japonicum revealed itself—a Far Eastern form of the worm that burrowed beneath the skin of its victims, then found its way to the walls of the intestine and rarely caused any symptoms until about five or six weeks later when it began producing eggs.

'An ELISA test will confirm it,' she told the doctor. 'It shows an increase in white blood cells, particularly eosinophils. A single dose of Praziquantel tablets is recommended,' she finished, reading the information triumphantly from the screen.

'Well done!' a deep voice said as she smiled at the doctor's thanks and dropped the phone back into its cradle.

Peter Wade was propped against the desk behind her.

'What made you think of bilharziasis?' he asked, sounding interested rather than officious, although contact between them, up until now, had been limited to formal 'good morning's or 'good afternoon's.

'I knew it was a danger for white-water enthusiasts on some of the rivers in Africa. Once he said gorge and kayaking, my brain started to click into gear.'

She smiled at him, still flushed and triumphant with the heady sense of victory.

He smile back—the old smile she remembered which sparked in his clear blue eyes and hovered on his lips like a blessing bestowed on only a rare few.

'I can see why Jan is impressed by her latest recruit,' he said. 'I've been away more than I've been at home these last few weeks but I keep hearing your praises sung whenever I step foot in the office.'

'That's silly,' she muttered, acutely embarrassed by this tribute. 'I'm only doing the job. She probably praises everyone who doesn't make a complete hash of it.'

She squirmed uncomfortably, as ill at ease as a teenager in the headmaster's office.

'Don't argue, Mel—Melanie!' he ordered softly, and his hand reached out and one finger pressed fleetingly against her lips—cool and soft against their heat.

The shrill of the phone broke the moment, and she saw him turn away to speak to Rose as she lifted the receiver and murmured, 'UniversAid, may I help you?'

It was a hospital in Atlantic City, New Jersey, reporting the admission of an Australian couple involved in a car accident. Were they definitely insured with one of the UniversAid-affiliated insurance companies and would the insurance cover their hospital bills?

'Could I have all the details, please?' Melanie asked.

Pulling out a clean file sheet, she jotted down names, insurance details, particulars of the hospital and attending doctor then moved on to injuries sustained.

'The husband has suffered fractures of the tibia and fibula in the right leg, with bruising of the spleen and possibly other internal damage. He's being monitored at the moment. The wife was four months pregnant and has aborted the foetus. She haemorrhaged badly but is now stable, although she's still heavily sedated.'

Pity clutched at Melanie's stomach as she finished her notes. 'If you could give me her name, I'll get back to you in a few minutes,' she said thickly, suprised at how affected she felt by an accident to strangers she would never meet.

'More trouble?' Peter asked, sliding into the chair beside her.

She pushed her sheet of notes across to him, while her fingers typed in the client name and insurance code number.

The details flashed up. Mr and Mrs Allen had a six-week Family Super cover—which was just as well, she thought, remembering the seven-thousand-dollar-a-day charges of some American intensive-care units. She jotted down the details, then turned back to Peter, who was frowing at the form.

'See if we have any details on this fellow either under his name or under the hospital,' he said jabbing his finger at the doctor's name on the new file.

Melanie left the couple's insurance information on the screen, and keyed in the command to open the next file on top of it. While the information search was under way, she watched Peter, amazed to see so clearly the working of his mind in subtle twitches of muscle beneath his cheek and the quick gathering of the skin between his brows.

'You're worried about something?' she prompted as she waited for the machine to respond to her latest request.

'I don't like the thought of that woman on her own over there. Neither of them can provide much support for the other, and she's a prime candidate for post-partum depression without her familiar network of friends and family.'

'Perhaps she has a relative who could fly over to be with her,' Melanie suggested, then pointed to the screen that had finally produced details of the doctor in Atlantic City, including surgery and after-hours phone numbers.

'See if you can get hold of him for me,' he said, 'then phone your contact person at the hospital and assure her about the cover. Ask if the couple's families have been contacted. If they have, then your contact may have some idea of their reaction.'

Dailling through the international code, she could hear Peter's frustrated muttering, and turned to him, an eyebrow raised in interrogation.

'I've been badgering the insurance companies to include cover for a relative to fly to an injured or ill patient,' he explained. 'It would often obviate the need for an expensive medical team to go, when hand-holding is all that's required.'

He sounded so cross she had to smile. He might be punctilious in his approach, but he was accustomed to getting his own way and the insurance companies' refusal to bend to his command was obviously frustrating him.

'Dr Reynolds' office.'

The American-accented voice was so clear, the woman could have been in the next room. Melanie explained who she was and passed on the fact that Peter would like to speak to Dr Reynolds.

'I'm not certain where he is at the moment, but give me your number, dear, and I'll page him and get him to call you "toot sweet!" Dr Wade, was it?'

The cheerful response made Melanie smile, and she carefully repeated the ITD and STD codes.

'He'll get back to you,' she said, the smile still lingering on her lips as she turned to Peter, surprising a frown of such ferocity that she wondered what she'd done wrong.

'Should I have given her your home number?' she quaked, watching as he shook his head, and his features relaxed into a rueful smile.

'No, I'll stay here until we have this sorted out,' he told her, but the *frisson* of alarm the frown had triggererd remained as a shadow behind her relief. Had he come in to check up on her?

Then he explained, as if answering her unspoken query. 'I flew back from Africa three days ago, and I find flying east seems to unbalance my body clock so badly that a normal sleep pattern is impossible for days afterwards. I come in here, rather than tossing and turning in bed.'

She nodded and dialled the hospital, her thoughts turning to the young couple, stranded far from home and suffering not only the pain of physical injuries, but the devastating loss of their unborn child as well.

'What do we do now?' she asked, after she had reassured the hospital accounts section that their patients' accounts would be paid. 'I've only dealt with cases where a family member or the insurance company has contacted us. Do we contact the family?'

'Wait till I've spoken to the attending physician,' Peter replied. 'It might be a good idea if you shift to the next work-space for a while. That way, we can keep the details of this case up on that computer screen without opening half a dozen files on top of it.'

'Will I write it up on the board?' she asked as she straightened up the desk, leaving only the new file on the top of it.

'When we know more, I think,' he replied, standing up from his chair and resting one hand lightly on her shoulder. 'I'll make us all coffee. How do you have it?'

She knew the gesture was a simple way of drawing her attention to his question, yet a warmth she could not understand burnt in the skin beneath his hand.

'Black with sugar,' she murmured, then sighed as he turned to ask Rose the same question, filling her in on the American case, before moving quietly out of the room.

Rose fielded the next call and spoke for a few minutes before calling across to her.

'It's a Mrs Armstrong on line three, Melanie. Her daughter is one of your accident victims in Atlantic City.'

Nerves she hadn't felt before in her telephone conversations dried her mouth, and she had to force herself to shift back to the computer station that held the details then to reach out and press the button that would put the call through to this extension. Was it a side-effect of working nights, this heightened tension she could feel tightening her body?

'We have spoken to the hospital,' she assured the agitated woman. 'They are receiving the very best of care, and will be fully covered for the cost of it.'

'It isn't the money that worries me, it's the baby. They've been married seven years, and always wanted a baby, but finally decided it wasn't meant to be. They put their energy into planning this trip around the States and they'd no sooner made all the arrangements and paid their deposit than Anna fell pregnant.'

There was a pause, then a muffled sound, as if tears were being hasily dispatched.

'She was in such good health, they decided to go ahead with the trip anyway!' Mrs Armstrong finished with a despairing break in her voice that told Melanie more than words. The grandchild had been as eagerly awaited as the child!

Stifling an urge to cry herself, she spoke calmly.

'An accident can happen anywhere, at any time,' she said soothingly. 'They could as easily have been driving to visit you. The most important thing is that they will both be OK, and that they are in good hands.'

There was a mumbled reply, and Melanie continued,

'Providing there's no permanent damage, there can be other babies, Mrs Armstrong. Let's be as positive as we can.'

'But she'll be so upset, all on her own over there, with him injured as well,' came the desperate response, and Melanie knew that no soothing words would cure this woman's despair.

'Dr Wade is in the office now,' she said, knowing that the more information the woman had, the easier it would be for her to cope. 'He's waiting for a phone call from Dr Reynolds in New Orleans who has seen them both.'

'It's too far away!' the woman sobbed, and Melanie wanted to leave the phone and go and sit beside her, an arm around her shoulders, to help her through the long night.

'I know that, but the distance isn't such a problem,' she said with a false heartiness. 'We can sit right here and summon up whatever specialist is required for your daughter and son-in-law, you know. Once Dr Wade has spoken to Dr Reynolds, he can decide if we need to call in more help, and also how long they will have to stay in hospital. It may be that, once they are stable enough to travel, we can bring them home and they can go into hospital here.'

'Can you do that?' the woman asked doubtfully, as if such a solution was beyond the scope of her imagination.

'It might be possible,' Melanie told her cautiously, unwilling to raise too much hope, but determined to give the woman something positive to consider. Winking lights on the phone warned her of two incoming calls.

'I have this number for you on our files, Mrs

Armstrong,' she said, reading out the contact phone number from the computer file to confirm it was still valid. 'I'll call you back as soon as Dr Wade has spoken to Dr Reynolds, and let you know what's happening.'

The hesitancy with which the woman said goodbye told Melanie that she would have liked to keep talking. It was as if the phone connection to UniversAid was a lifeling to hope to which she was clinging, a cord connecting her to the daughter she could not reach and comfort.

Ignoring an impulse to accede to the unspoken request, she ended the call with a final assurance then fielded the first of the incoming calls, shifting to the next chair as she realised it was not connected with the case in Atlantic City.

Peter returned and placed her coffee and saucer of biscuits on the desk beside her, then slipped into the chair she had vacated to take the second call still winking its insistence from the phone.

While she passed on the name of an English-speaking doctor in Bonn to a concerned businessman in Germany, she could hear Peter enquiring about the Allens, asking the questions that would enable him to make decisions for their welfare although they were thousands of miles away.

'Most of the larger hotels can recommend English-speaking doctors,' she told the agitated man at the end of the phone, who was running through the rest of his itinerary and demanding the name and address of a suitable medico at each of his stop-overs.

'I don't wish to discuss my personal business with hotel staff,' he told her angrily.

'Would you like to speak to a doctor here?' she asked, hoping to calm him. Although the medical officers on the staff rarely did shifts in the office, there was always one on call and phone calls could be transferred to him for a long-distance consultation.

She was wondering if Peter would speak to the man, since he was here, when the slight hesitancy between question and answer that typified the overseas connection was broken by an abrupt denial of need.

'I simply want to be prepared in case of an emergency,' the belligerent voice replied, and Melanie wondered if perhaps this man was as uncertain and upset as Mrs Armstrong, clinging to a line stretching from his lonely hotel room, home.

She brought up the cities he'd listed and proceeded to give him the names and phone numbers he wanted, and was relieved when he finally thanked her civilly and said goodbye.

She picked up the coffee and sipped at it gratefully, feeling the sugary sweetness hit her system. Not a medically recommended booster, she knew, but the combination of carbohydrate and caffeine worked wonders on her metabolism, which had begun protesting that it was time for her to sleep.

Beside her, she heard Peter saying thank you to his caller, and turned enquiringly towards him.

'A gynaecologist has examined Mrs Allen, and she's had an ultrasound. There doesn't appear to be any internal damage but she's suffered a massive blood loss and was hypovolemic when brought in.'

'She was lucky they diagnosed it, with the increase in blood volume that occurs in early pregnancy,' Melanie said, shaking her head as her mind followed the woman's progress.

'It appears she was conscious and her first thoughts were for the baby.' He paused and Melanie looked up from the notes she was adding to the businessman's file to find his eyes on her, his face still. 'She'd have known she was miscarrying,' he added quietly. 'Even at four months, the force of the seatbelt cutting across her abdomen could trigger a spontaneous abortion.'

Disconcerted by something she couldn't understand in his voice, she nodded her understanding.

'I suppose we should be glad it isn't worse than that,' Melanie responded, and explained about the longed-for baby.

'We shouldn't be glad or sad,' he told her firmly, the autocratic 'Englishness' back in his voice. 'That's personal involvement, which, as you should know, is not recommended for the medical profession.'

'If we didn't care about people, we'd be engineers or sheet-metal workers,' Melanie told him sharply, angered by his denial of involvement.

'And you don't argue all the time?' One eyebrow rose in a teasing query that made Melanie's heart turn over. There was something about this man that left her feeling curiously defenceless.

'And Mr Allen? What's the word on him?' she asked, ignoring his bait as she forced her mind back to work matters. She hoped she sounded sufficiently detached to satisfy his idea of medical propriety.

'He was suffering abdominal pain, and they considered performing a peritoneal lavage when they anaesthetised him prior to the surgery on his leg, but decided, as he was going to be conscious and in hospital, they could monitor his vital functions closely enough to identify any changes.'

'I suppose if there were signs of internal bleeding they'd have gone ahead with it,' Melanie said, trying to

understand what he was telling her. 'Is there some
other way they can check on internal damage?'

'CAT scans could identify subcapsular injuries to the
liver and spleen if there are any signs that it's
necessary.'

'So what do we do next?'

'We, Melanie?' he asked, confusing her completely
with a curious cadence in the words.

'UniversAid,' she replied with dignity, refusing to
join in some game she did not understand, particularly
when his mere presence in the operations-room was
causing her to feel an uncharacteristic uncertainty.

'We wait,' he said softly. 'If they're planning an
extended visit to the States it may be that they would
opt to stay on in hospital over there, until they're well
enough to continue their journey. In a case like that,
our flying them home could severely disrupt their
future plans.'

'But it was a six-week insurance cover, dated from
five weeks ago,' Melanie told him.

'You've already checked?' He sounded surprised,
but went on explaining in his quiet voice. 'The length
of cover always gives us a clue, and we get additional
information from the family, if that's available. A set
time usually means they have taken holidays from
work, and need to be back by a certain day. I suppose
we can assume they were on the last leg of their trip,
possibly intending to end up in New York for the flight
home.'

He was speaking with a calm concentration, but she
could see the frown gathering his eyebrows together
again, and wondered what was nagging at his mind. As
if preoccupied by his own uneasy thoughts, he gathered
up her cup, then rose and walked out of the room.

Picking up the Allens' file, she noticed the notes he had added to it and was pleased to see that his writing was decipherable. The phones were quiet, giving her time to walk across and write up the particulars of the two cases on the whiteboard, allotting each a separate case number, and filling in the necessary details with particular care.

Whoever was on duty when the next communication came from Atlantic City, the outline would be there for them, and the reference they would need to access the case in the computer files was clearly visible.

Now she had to transfer the information from the written file to the computer. She moved back to the desk, then remembered Mrs Armstrong. How much of what they knew should she pass on to the anxious mother?

'What would you do, Rose?' she asked as she finished explaining the situation and her promise to phone back.

'Ask Peter,' said Rose promptly.

'But if he hadn't been in tonight, I'd have had to handle it myself,' she argued, unwilling to appear inadequate in front of him.

'But he is here tonight, and as he's already taken on the case I'm sure he'll be the doctor following it through. It's certainly up to him from now on to decide what families are told.'

It made sense, she decided, but that didn't make it any easier to go through to his office and speak to him. It must be the effect of this, her first night shift, that was throwing things out of proportion!

The phones were still silent, so she scribbled Mrs Armstrong's phone number on a message slip and forced herself to stand up and walk across the room.

At the door, she debated ringing Mrs Armstrong and
telling her that all was well. They would probably not
have any more news until the next day, but the
woman's anxiety had been patently obvious, and such
blanket reassurances were certain to sound false.

Peering through the glass wall of Peter's office, she
could see the back of his dark head as his chair was
swung away from the desk, facing towards a low set of
bookshelves. It wasn't until she was inside the room
that she realised he was asleep, the chair tilted back
and his long legs stretched out, heels resting on the
bookshelves.

Curiosity drew her forward, until she was close
enough to reach out and touch him. Her eyes moved
hungrily over his face, taking in the pale lines radiating
from his eyes and the grey pallor of tiredness beneath
the clear, tight skin.

He was breathing lightly and easily, his well-shaped
lips relaxed slightly so that a glimpse of white teeth
made him appear to be smiling. Long, dark lashes
threw feathery shadows on to his cheeks, matching the
straggle of dark hair that had flopped on to his forehead. She resisted an impulse to smooth it back, to
press her fingers against the pulse she could see throb-
bing at his temple.

Get out of here, her mind commanded, but her legs
were reluctant to obey. Her heartbeats accelerated,
and her fingers ached with the control she was exerting
to stop them moving towards him. . .

The sudden buzzing of the phone brought her back
to her senses, and, although it was quickly silenced and
she guessed that Rose had picked it up in the control-
room, she hurried away, deciding to phone Mrs
Armstrong and give her an outline of what Peter had

learned, and assure her that someone would be in touch if there was any change.

It was the briefest of calls, as the phones had come to life, but she confirmed that the Allens were at the end of their visit and that both families would prefer to have them back at home.

Then all thoughts of individual personalities were banished as she worked methodically through the requests, complaints and explanations of tour leaders, travellers, relatives and overseas insurance agents that were the bulk of the work covered by UniversAid.

'It's only a matter of time before the night-shift phone staff is expanded to three or four,' Rose remarked as they took advantage of a lull in the telephonic demands to eat the sandwiches they'd brought in for 'lunch'.

'Is the business still growing, then?' Melanie asked, uncertain about the history of the company.

'Is it ever!' Rose replied. 'I only do telephones—I've got kids at school and can't be flitting around the world all the time—but in two years I've seen it grow from twenty staff to the forty-seven we have now. That includes the six doctors, of course, who don't work for us full-time but are all rostered to be on call and are also available for repatriation work.'

Was there a limit to how big the service could grow? Melanie wondered, lifting the receiver to her ear again, the fingers of her free hand hovering over the computer keyboard.

'Mel, it's me, Kip,' the voice whispered, and alarm spurted through Melanie as she demanded,

'What are you doing ringing me at——' she checked her watch '—one-thirty in the morning?'

'It's Barry. He called in at about eleven and wanted

to know where you were. He'd obviously been drinking
and didn't believe me when I said you were at work.'

'I'm sorry you've had this bother,' Melanie told her,
speaking as quietly as she could into the phone in an
effort to disguise the fact that this was a personal call.
'Did you get rid of him?'

'No,' Kip muttered softly. 'That's why I'm ringing. I
didn't want him to get back into his car and drive
anywhere—he could have killed himself——'

'Or someone else,' Melanie interrupted angrily.

'Yes, well. . .' There was another long pause. 'I told
him he could stay,' Kip finished. 'In fact, I've finally
got him to bed in your room, and I'm ringing to say
you'd better crash on the couch when you get home. I
thought a stray body in the bed might freak you out
after your first night shift.'

'Thanks, Kip,' Melanie said with rueful gratitude.
She knew there was nothing else Kip could have done,
but Barry was a problem she didn't want to have to
handle when he woke up in the morning. Asleep on
the couch, she'd make a prime target for his list of
imagined grievances or litany of love—the choice
depending on his mood!

She was mulling over her own stupidity in befriend-
ing Barry on her flight back from Botswana, when
Peter Wade walked back into the room. Had he ever
arrived at Cynthia's flat drunkenly professing his love?
She shook her head. Definitely not a scenario she could
envisage, she decided, smiling at her own flighty
thoughts.

'I think we'll go over and get the Allens,' he said, as
if they had been discussing this only moments earlier.
'I've got a nasty feeling about it, and the sooner we can
get there the better.'

'We' as in UniversAid? Melanie wondered. Surely that was what he meant although he was looking at her as if he was waiting for her to respond to some personal invitation.

'I'll get the airline schedules and see what flights depart early in the morning,' Rose responded before Melanie could ask what to do next. 'Have you checked the roster to see who's available?'

'Have I?' Peter responded with a wry shake of his head. 'We seem to have had a rash of incidents lately. I want someone with O and G experience, and Dave's taken that woman back to Hong Kong, Jan's flying in from Switzerland tomorrow, Fred's on holiday, so guess who's left?'

'But you're just back, Peter,' Rose protested, while Melanie read about the other cases he'd mentioned on the board.

'I've been back three days. That's more time than we get on turn-arounds. Get two seats on the first available flight to anywhere in the States,' Peter told her. 'We can take something internal from wherever we arrive. Once I've assessed the situation, I'll call Bill and he can organise the trip home.'

'Easier said than done if you've got to cross the States,' Rose reminded him as she hurried out of the room.

'Your relief comes on at five, that right?' Peter asked, ignoring Rose's words as he turned to Melanie. She nodded.

His face was creased in thought, but the tiredness she'd seen earlier was gone and an air of excitement emanated from him, as if he had picked up the scent of the chase and was burning with an eagerness to get on

with it. A glimpse of the adventurer she remembered
shone through the polished exterior.

'If we can get on an early flight out of Brisbane, I'll
run you home to get your things, or follow you home if
your car is here, then we can go straight to the airport.'

'We?'

The word came out like a strangled yelp.

'You and I,' he said patiently. 'We'll go to America
and bring the Allens home.'

'But I'm still on trial,' Melanie objected, although
her heart was fluttering with a quite unreasonable
excitement.

'Believe me, I know that only too well. If I'd had
any alternatives, you'd have been the last one I'd have
chosen, but as things have turned out, what better way
to test your mettle than a field exercise?' he replied,
his lips twisting into an indecipherable smile. 'Now, get
cracking and print out all the information we have on
the case, and while that's happening get on to Mrs
Allen's mother and tell her we're almost on our way.'

'It's nearly two a.m.,' she reminded him, and was
rewarded with a broad, genuine smile.

'I don't hink she'll mind being woken to be told
we're going,' he assured her. 'She might have a special
message for the pair of them, and should also be able
to suggest the best hospital for them back here. They're
from Melbourne, aren't they?'

Melanie gaped at him, unable to believe that this
could be happening. She had applied for her US visa
on joining the company, as even probationary staff
were required to keep this authorisation current, but
she had never imagined being called on to use it so
soon.

'You might also check the file for Mr Allen's next of

kin and let them know we're off. The office will be in touch with both families and organise things for our arrival back here, once I've assessed the situation over there.'

She could hear the words and see his lips moving, but her mind was not processing the information. All she could think of was Kip saying 'You've always said you'd like a chance to have that part of your life over again'.

'Get cracking, Melly,' he said, and walked away before she could protest at his use of the childish diminutive, or fully comprehend that once again she would be taking a long plane journey with this stranger. And, once again, he did not want her with him!

Would she be able to prove herself on this mission? And could she expunge the memories of her behaviour eight years ago?

She typed in the code number of the Allens' file and keyed in the print command, then lifted the phone to contact Mrs Armstrong, her mind on automatic pilot while the past and the present collided with such force that she found it difficult to think.

CHAPTER THREE

EDUARDO CASEL had been twenty-one, slim, dark and dreamily handsome to the seventeen-year-old Melanie on her first foray away from parental guidance and care. The son of her host family on the student exchange programme, his status as a third-year university student had enhanced his standing in her love-struck eyes, and she had hung on every word he said, openly adoring, swept up in the delightful pain, the exquisite torment, of first love.

She dialled a number and heard Mrs Armstrong express relief, delight and gratitude. The printer by the wall clacked out its information, but Melanie's mind was entangled in the sticky web of the past, as fragments of memory flashed on an inner screen, clear as holiday slides.

Eduardo had been skilful. She had acknowledged that some years ago, when time and maturity had enabled her to look back to her stay in Portugal with understanding and bring the shadows of guilt and horror out into the open. The exercise had been similar to talking about a nightmare in order to reduce its fearsomeness to manageable proportions, and it had helped to bring the past into truer perspective.

Eduardo had not only accepted her adoration, but fed it with subtle touches, brushing past her in the cool corridors of his home, casting meaningful glances at her while they dined, and letting his fingers linger too long in hers as they greeted or parted from each other.

These hidden messages had fired her adolescent body to a frenzy of desire, feeding her rampaging hormones until she'd hungered for him with an aching need that had blotted out her common sense, all thoughts of consequences, and the moral values that were inherent to her upbringing.

The actual consummation of the madness, made more sordid by the fact that it was in a dusty attic directly above the room where his parents slept, had been a painful affront to all her senses, a shattering of the fragile illusion of love. Eduardo's rough force had shocked her and the reality of the physical act of love had left her feeling sick, ashamed and desperately unhappy.

Cessation of noise told her that the printer had stopped, and she hurried across to it and tore off the information, then concentrated on the printed words, checking that all the information they would need was there. The past must be put behind her! This was her opportunity to show Peter Wade that the Melly Ashcroft he had brought home eight years ago was dead and buried, and in her place was Melanie—efficient, calm and capable—a perfect employee for UniversAid!

'And who the hell is that?' the man she was trying to impress demanded a few hours later. He was speaking in a harsh whisper, having drifted silently behind her into her bedroom, clutching the overnight bag she'd dragged out of the hall cupboard.

Melanie's heart quaked. She'd forgotten all about Barry!

'It's a friend of Kip's—staying over. She put him in here because I was on night duty.' She blurted out the

first thing that came into her head, hoping the heat she
felt as she told the lie was not visible in the shaft of
light spearing in from the hall.

Pulling open her underwear drawer, she grabbed at
the first sets she could find. No need to take too much
when she could wash them out at the hotel. A pair of
pyjamas was added to the selection, then a spare pair
of jeans, three T-shirts, and an uncrushable skirt.

'Do I have time for a quick shower?' she asked,
taking the bag from him and folding in the clothes,
adding her running shorts and a pair of joggers.

'Certainly,' Peter told her, his eyes still straying to
the figure in the bed. 'I'll make us a cup of tea if that's
OK.'

Melanie nodded and pointed him towards the
kitchen then hurried into the small bathroom that was
sandwiched between her and Kip's bedrooms.

She heard the voices in the kitchen as she emerged,
her wet hair clinging damply to her head and her
hairdrier and toilet bag clutched in her hand.

'We've no time for hair-drying,' Peter snapped at
her, and she spun around to face him, seeing the clear
expression of distaste on his face before she caught a
glimpse of Barry hovering sheepishly in the kitchen
behind him.

'I wasn't intending to dry it,' she told him calmly,
although a wave of nausea was sweeping through her
body. Getting caught out in a lie is a great way to
prove your worthiness as an employee, her conscience
needled, as she rammed the dryer and other last minute
essentials into her small carry-on bag.

'I'm sorry about last night,' Barry said, carrying her
cup of tea through into the living-room and looking at
her with the eyes of a mournful spaniel.

Melanie took the cup from him, the familiar exasperation she felt at his refusal to accept friend status biting like acid at her nerve-endings.

'It's Kip you should be apologising to,' she told him curtly, thinking of her friend's tired voice during the one o'clock phone call. She crossed the room to remove her passport from a desk drawer and tuck it safely into her handbag.

'I wouldn't bother keeping up that pretence,' Peter said coolly as he came into the room, obviously anxious to be off. 'Barry has told me about your trip to Africa.'

And made it sound as if we went away together, Melanie thought savagely, feeling far more dismay and anger than was logical. And what business of Peter Wade's was her personal life anyway? She gulped at her tea, feeling it searing down her throat.

'I'm ready, so let's go,' she said, putting down the half-empty cup and picking up the warm but light windproof jacket that accompanied her everywhere she went. She was trying desperately to regain the poise that had won his compliment only hours earlier, but the senseless lie niggled beneath her skin—like a bilharziasis-carrying worm! she thought savagely.

'But I need to talk to you,' Barry bleated.

'There's nothing to talk about, Barry,' she said firmly, then realised how heartless she must sound to someone who hadn't heard her say it a hundred times before.

With a quick good bye flung over her shoulder, she led the way out of the door, her spine stiffening when she heard Peter's taunting, 'Not much of a farewell for your boyfriend.'

'He is not my boyfriend,' she told him through clenched jaws, while he unlocked the car door for her.

'Dropped him after the trip to Africa?' he pursued, holding the door open for her with his usual unnerving courtesy.

'There was no trip to Africa, not the way he makes it sound,' she stormed, furious that the harmony she had felt between them earlier had been shattered by this pointless conversation. 'You've heard Barry's version, but the actual fact of the matter is that we came home on the same flight.'

The urge to slam the door on his needling practically overwhelmed her. Perhaps that was why he'd held it, she thought savagely as he shut it with a gentle click and walked around the front of the car.

'Well, it's none of my business anyway,' he told her calmly as he slid in behind the wheel.

The comment made her want to grind her teeth in fury. Of course it was none of his business, so why bring it up? Why question her in the first place?

'I did warn you that this job is hard on relationships,' he added, as if to stir the embers of her wrath.

She could see his long fingers steady on the wheel—capable hands, she thought, then glanced at his face to see if he'd caught her looking at them. His attention was fixed on the road, his angular profile revealing absolutely nothing.

'I do not have relationships,' she told him, hoping the firmness in her voice would put an end to the confusing conversation.

'Everyone has relationships,' he said pedantically. 'With friends and family, as well as with lovers.'

The last word struck a discordant note in her mind. He'd assumed the 'no-hopers' had been her lovers, she remembered, and she'd done nothing to deny the assumption. Her sheer bloody-mindedness at the time had probably prompted her to exaggerate the closeness of the little band, although the eight young men she'd met up with in the square as Cascais had treated her like a sister.

'I don't have lovers, then,' she said stoutly, trying to repel the new wave of memories with this frank denial.

'Beautiful girl like you, big brown bedroom eyes, hair that holds the morning sun captive in its thick waves—of course you must have lovers. Or are you saying there's no one holding the position at the moment, apart from the luckless Barry?'

Bedroom eyes? For a moment she was tempted to put this increasingly bizarre conversation down to some kind of waking dream occurring in her mind because of the sleepless night, but a quick glance at her interrogator's profile was enought to tell her he was real, and the stern set of his lips suggested this was not the light banter it might have passed for in different circumstances.

It must be another test, she decided—a spot of provocation to see if she would react in an over-emotional way and he could prove her fallible under pressure.

'We're all different, Dr Wade,' she said primly, hoping to turn the conversation back to him. 'And I was taught not to judge other people by myself.'

The car had swept into the çar park of a tall block of apartments at St Lucia. On the river, Melanie decided, thinking about the route they had taken from her flat at Toowong.

It slid to a halt in one of the visitors' parking bays, and Peter pulled on the handbrake and turned to her with a teasing smile.

'Sheath your claws, little kitten,' he murmured, his

eyes meeting hers with a strangely rueful gleam in their blueness. 'And call me Peter. Will you come up while I throw a few things together and have a quick shower?'

Melanie nodded, confused by the shift in the atmosphere from cold testiness to warm complicity. Maybe he had decided to make the best of things, she decided. After all, they would be stuck with each other for company for the next few days.

She climbed out of the car and followed him, aware of a certain light-headedness that she put down to lack of sleep.

'I find it's often easier on staff who've been on night shift to take these early international flights. Their bodies are ready to sleep, not all fired up wanting to get on with the day,' he told her as they entered a beautiful foyer, floored in marble, and decorated with tall, healthy plants in brass containers, and low white armchairs.

Was he feeling the same curious detachment as she was, she wondered, that he'd shifted the conversation abruptly back to business?

'As long as I make it to the plane before my body sleeps,' she said as the lift whipped them silently up to the tenth floor.

'I imagine sheer stubborn pride would insist on it,' he responded calmly, making her look quickly into his face to see if she could detect a hidden meaning behind the words.

Eight years ago he'd labelled her the most stubborn, argumentative, wayward specimen of human nature it had ever been his misfortune to meet. She remembered the words as clearly as if he were speaking them now!

He was watching the lift doors open, face blandly still, his mind probably in Atlantic City as the cogs of the operation he had started began turning smoothly through the complicated process of retrieval.

He led her into a carpeted lobby, then unlocked the unit door on the right and ushered her through, waving a hand towards the heavy leather armchairs that were turned side-on to the wide windows.

'Give me ten minutes,' he said, and Melanie drifted across the room, perversely resistant, now she was here, to seeing this place where he lived with Cynthia. Small signs of marital harmony would be too much to handle in her present tired and faintly bemused state, she decided, and focused on the view beyond the wall of glass.

Although the sun had not yet risen, the light of dawn had crept ahead of it, and the scene before her was a muted tapestry of silver, black and grey.

Directly below her, the river flowed, its movement indiscernible, so that it lay like a broad, silver arc— shining mercury spilled across a landscape. Beyond it, the trees on the opposite bank were still darkly shadowed, black guardians of the magic metallic strip. Above them, houses teetered up the steep banks, one-dimensional in the vague light, like geometric shapes stuck on a collage.

Her eyes held the beauty but her mind drifted as purposefully as the unseen movement of the river.

Eight years ago, she'd told Peter Wade she loved him, translating all her fear and confusion into an emotion she craved, transferring her hero-worshipping heart from the betrayer to the saviour. She'd sorted that all out in her mind, too, when she'd relived the episode in her mind much later, and understood the reactions of the teenager she'd been.

But was enough of the past still with her to explain

the ambivalence she felt in Peter's presence? Was what
she felt today simply an undiscarded remnant of that
torridly overwrought emotion?

'OK, let's check things.'

She spun around, brought abruptly back to the
present by the casual words.

He was wearing a dark suit that must be made of the
new microfibre, moulding softly to his frame, elegantly
correct. Power-dressing! Of course he'd have to wear a
suit, she realised—too late—as she glanced now at her
own clean but faded jeans and flowered shirt. Staff at
hospitals expected their senior consultants to be correctly attired, and reacted to them accordingly. He
would command respect without opening his mouth.

'One of our dirvers will meet us at the airport with
the equipment case. Jan probably showed it to you. It
has things like the Oxylog, catheters, bottles, IV equipment, and some broad-spectrum drugs always packed
in it. I've money and credit cards, and you and I both
have our passports,' he said oblivious to the new
embarrassment that was twisting her stomach.

He patted his pocket and cocked an enquiring eyebrow at her, all business now, as if the prying personal
questions had never been asked, and her choice of
clothing was of no importance.

Be practical, Melanie, she urged herself, grateful
that she'd thrown in that one skirt almost as an
afterthought.

'Do we take stretchers?' she asked, remembering the
different collapsible models she'd seen in the store
cupboard and matching his professionalism with her
own stumbling effort.

'I'm hoping we won't need them on this trip. If we
do, the airline companies we're likely to fly with on

our way home have basic stretchers we can use in emergencies, and all have wheelchairs, so, unless we know we can't get one where we're going, or need the special spinal stretcher, we don't bother to take our own.'

Melanie followed him out of the unit, Cynthia forgotten as she sensed something more behind the words.

'What did Rose mean about it being easier said than done crossing the United States?' she asked as they waited for the lift.

Peter grinned at her, and she felt a flush of warmth course through her tired body.

'Don't miss much, do you?' he said, ushering her through the opening doors, and sending the small capsule slipping downwards again. 'We have a few problems in the United States, flying patients who are dependent on just about anything.'

He watched her as he spoke, and she tried to look intelligent, although the constant togetherness and her dismay over her clothes were tugging at her nerve-endings and disrupting her thought processes.

'For legal reasons, airlines in the States would prefer we use an air ambulance, but the cost is often prohibitive. Litigation is practically a national sport over there, and the airlines are understandably reluctant to carry patients with drips protruding from their bodies, or with lungs relying on a ventilator.'

They were walking back towards his car now, and she moved a little apart and breathed in the fresh morning air.

'If Mrs Allen is on intravenous antibiotics, which is likely after the miscarriage, how do we get around it?' she asked.

'It's a good trip for you to learn the ropes on,' Peter

told her, a certain satisfaction in his tone. 'You'll soon find out what we do if the need arises!'

It was an unsatisfactory answer. *Does he think I won't need to know, if he's going to sack me at the end of the two-month trial?* The thought triggered a miserable little skip in the steady beating of her heart. Then she was back in the car and his body was again assaulting hers with that silent, unseen, seductive blend of past and present.

Perhaps she'd have to walk away herself at the end of the trial! Unless she could get rid of the stray fancies the man provoked, it would be the safest route to take, no matter how much she loved the job.

The airport provided the normal scene of organised chaos, firing Melanie's nerves with excited anticipation. The UniversAid driver had already checked their medical baggage through to Philadelphia, and he handed over the baggage-claim tickets.

'You've been upgraded to first class for the first leg to Honolulu,' he explained, and Melanie cringed. Flying first class for the first time in her life, and she was wearing her oldest, most comfortable jeans!

'Why would the airline do that?' she bleated, shaking her head as she realised how little she knew about the service.

'It's Qantas,' Peter replied, as if that explained everything. 'We fly with them whenever possible because, as our national airline, they are also concerned with the welfare of Australian tourists abroad and will do whatever they can to help us bring them home. We book business class,' he continued, 'and if there are spare seats up front they usually upgrade us. It makes it a bit easier to get the sleep you need to keep going.'

*   *   *

'Sleep well?' Peter's voice pierced the foggy mists of confusion. Melanie looked around. She remembered settling into the wide first-class seat as the plane had taken off from Brisbane, remembered Peter's smile and the way he'd said, 'Well, we're off again, Melly,' making her feel as if she was eighteen again. Everything beyond that was a compete blank.

'You were right about night-duty staff sleeping on the flights,' she said, smiling shyly at her boss while she wondered how ruffled and untidy she looked. 'Have you slept?'

He nodded, a smile playing at the corner of his lips. The smile was reflected in his eyes, and it unsettled her with its. . .intimacy? She had barely settled on this bizarre possibility when it was banished by his next words, all practicality!

'You've time for a wash before they serve lunch. We go through Customs and Immigration at Hawaii, change to an American Airlines flight through to Dallas, then change again for Philadelphia.'

'You sound as casual as if we're taking a bus into town,' Melanie objected, her own bubbling excitement chasing away the shadows of sleep and its attendant confusion as names of places she had only read of dropped from his tongue.

'Oh, I'm excited,' he said, and smiled again, as if he was sharing some very special secret with her.

Her physical reaction to the smile was so extreme, she pulled herself hurriedly out of the seat and stepped over his legs, heading for the washroom as swiftly as her trembling legs would take her. Apart from being her boss, he was a married man! She *must* stop reacting to every smile like a teenager on a first date.

Inside the small cubicle, she splashed water on her

face, scrubbing her hands across it as if the effort could
wash away the thoughts that rioted beneath her skull.
She brushed her hair back into a semblance of tidiness,
wondering at his earlier description. She thought of it
as almost fair, the sun-bleached streaks lightening the
gentle shade of mouse!

'Hair that holds the morning sun in its thick waves,'
he had said!

She brushed her hand over the thickness, and smiled
at her reflection. Even if he didn't mean it, a compliment was always welcome.

Between Honolulu and Dallas, Peter told stories of
some of the cases they had handled, explaining how
much of their work involved the repatriation of elderly
people coming out to Australia to visit sons or daugh-
ters who had emigrated many years earlier.

'There is often such a great cultural difference
between the old home and the new that parents are
shocked, and become prime targets for heart attacks or
strokes,' he explained.

'That's a dreadful way for something that should be
as joyful as a family reunion to end,' Melanie said,
unable to hide her dismay.

'A truly dispassionate statement,' Peter teased, but
the smile that still hovered round his lips told her he
understood how she felt. He expanded on his explanation carefully.

'I think the older generation are impressed by their
offspring's obvious success, the big house and shiny
new car—things many people, in south-east Asia particularly, would only dream of owning. The disappointment is with their children's lifestyle.'

The statement puzzled Melanie. 'Aren't houses and
cars part of that lifestyle?'

'Yes, but it's the things that are missing from it, not what they have, that distress the older generation most. Many of our immigrants drop their reigious observances, and allow their children a freedom unheard of in their native land. The old people see it as a deterioration and express their disappointment, and the young ones can't understand, because materially they have achieved much more than they could ever hope to achieve back home.'

'A no-win situation?' Melanie said as she realised the barriers this would erect within the family.

'Precisely! It leads to arguments and fights that have no resolution. We took an elderly Vietnamese gentleman back to Ho Chi Minh City recently. He had suffered a heart attack, and his doctors suspected he'd had a mild stroke as well, because he simply stopped talking.'

Peter shuffled in his seat as he spoke, his arm brushing against Melanie's hand. Cautiously, she moved it to her lap, shrinking into her own space to keep away from his distracting movements.

'When he refused, or was unable, to talk to his son, the hospital brought in interpreters, hoping that it was all some misunderstanding. He showed no sign of understanding them—or of being able to reply—and it was decided that he was aphasic and that it would be best to take him home.'

'But would he have wanted to go back? Couldn't his family have kept him here?'

'We didn't know, is the answer to your first question, and no, the answer to the second. He was on a visitor's visa; he had to go, legally.'

'Well, that doesn't seem right,' Melanie muttered,

forgetting about Peter's nearness as she fretted about
an old, frail man begin sent away from his family.

'It's the law, Melanie,' he replied, smiling at her
pouting face. 'It was also the correct thing to do. He
was too old to transplant to foreign soil, and his body
knew that, probably before his mind did. We took him
home to a little shack in a rabbit warren of a street,
and he started babbling away to his friends, obviously
enthralling them with all the wonders he had seen, but
so pleased to be home, his happiness shone out of him
like a beacon.'

'But that's a lovely story!' she cried, turning towards
him with her pleasure as transparent as the old man's.

'A lot of them are,' he murmured. His eyes seemed
transfixed on her face, at first mirroring her own smile
with that soft gleam she'd surprised in them once
before, then slowly changing to a wide, blank blueness.
As the accompanying smile faded, and the suggestion
of a frown began, Melanie felt the cold chill of rejec-
tion, and turned away, pulling a magazine out of the
seat pocket in front of her with fingers that shook
uncontrollably.

'We should try to get some more sleep,' he said, his
voice now devoid of all emotion. 'We'll have a long
day ahead of us when we eventually reach mainland
America.'

At Dallas they had a two-hour wait for their next
flight, and, after depositing their hand baggage and
Melanie's jacket in a locker, they walked around the
vast terminal, working the stiffness out of their leg
muscles, and trying to orient their bodies to the time
changes.

'You could set out a good jogging track in this place
without leaving air-conditioned comfort,' Melanie

pointed out as they completed their first exploration of the public corridors, breaking the silence that was making her feel uneasy.

'You jog?' he asked, in such a disbelieving tone that Melanie chuckled.

'Is it against the rules?' she teased, pausing in her progress to turn towards him.

'No, it's an excellent way of keeping fit for young people, and physical fitness is essential in this business.' He shook his head, eyes skimming over her rounded hips and full bust. 'You don't seem like the jogging type.'

'Well, imagine how fat I'd be if I didn't jog,' she retorted, made edgy by the unseen chemistry that arced between them with his appraisal. Did he feel it too, or was it only on her side, this uneasiness when they were together, the sense of being a little bit more alive, or alert, or aware, not to mention downright uncomfortable when the conversation veered towards anything personal?

'I can't imagine you fat, either,' he said, shaking his head as if denying some image in his mind. And, as the smile that accompanied the words curled into her heart, Melanie broke up the uneasy hiatus by striding away.

Why should her body react to every smile, every nuance in his speech, as if it imagined he was flirting with her? He was a married man, securely fastened to Cynthia's side if her memories of Cynthia were to be trusted. And she wasn't interested in relationships anyway, she reminded herself, stretching her pace as if danger lurked behind the laggard. Particularly not in the unsatisfactory kind of relationship a married man could offer.

She looked back, and realised he wasn't following.

Now her musing shortened her stride and slowed her feet. Anyway, apart from her own objections to what she considered illicit affairs, it was highly unlikely that he saw her as anything other than the tiresome adolescent he'd once repatriated.

She wheeled into a long arcade of shops, built to tempt the bored transit passenger with bright windows and lavish goods. She must have lost Peter back where they'd paused, but there was another hour before their flight would be called and she was close enough to the departure lounge.

She sauntered along, looking idly into the windows in the hope of spying something special that she could take home to her parents or Kip.

The suit hung on a whip-slim model behind a display of wooden beads. It's knee-length skirt crossed over at the front, and had tiny gathers at the waistline, allowing a certain roominess despite its straight shape. It was a rich tobacco colour, and had a matching, long-sleeved jacket, its straight lines dropping to the model's hips. Beneath it, the clever window-dresser had added a blouse that was a riot of autumn colour—gold, burnt orange, umber and tan—swirling around in an asymmetric pattern.

Mentally, Melanie tried her beige silk blouse under the suit, and nodded in satisfaction, then envisaged the gold T-shirt she had packed, with the skirt, and decided it would be correctly informal.

She ventured inside the shop. Would the price be prohibitive?

'I'm booked on a flight that leaves in an hour,' she told the assistant, who had whipped the suit and blouse off the model in seconds and was ushering her into a booth.

I won't think about the cost, she vowed, when she saw the transformation from scruffy kid to sophisticate. She had her Mastercard and would pay it off if it took her the rest of her life!

'Will it crush?' she asked the assistant, and listened to voluble praise of the miracle fibre used in the suit. 'I'll take it,' she declared, when she could edge in the words.

Refusing to allow her mind to translate the American dollars back to Australian, she asked the woman to pack it for her, and handed over her card, her fingers clammy with excitement.

'Been spending your travel allowance?' Peter asked, when she arrived back at the departure lounge to find him waiting with their bags and her jacket.

'I didn't know we got one,' she replied, smiling up at him as the delight she still felt flowed over to embrace the world.

'You get a little extra to cover odds and ends,' he said, 'although expenses like hotel bills, meals and car hire are usually put on the company credit card.'

Her fascination with the service overcame her personal unease, and she forgot even the new suit as question after question occurred to her.

'Hire cars? Should I have an international licence? And what happens in places where they don't take credit cards? And could I sign a company card? I——'

'Whoa, Neddy!' Peter threw up his hands in surrender, laughing at the eager barrage of questions his few words of explanation had unleashed. 'Let's get back on the plane and I'll do my best to answer all your queries before we arrive in Philadelphia.'

He herded her towards the expandable tunnel leading on to the plane. 'To start with, we usually hire a

car and driver. Trying to find your way from hotel to
hospital in a strange town after a long flight would be
sheer folly. UniversAid try to make their couriers' jobs
as easy as possible!'

His head was bent so that his voice came from over
her shoulder, and she could feel his breath warm
against her cheek.

If you're not interested in an affair with a married
man, why did you buy the suit? her mind shouted as
the warmth sent shivers down her spine and reduced
her knees to sponge-like softness. She stopped in her
tracks, then responded mechanically to his shove from
behind, shocked that her subconscious could have
directed her into such folly!

CHAPTER FOUR

As the plane lifted back into the sky, Melanie concentrated on the view of Dallas, spread beneath them like a fabulous Lego construction. She was here to learn the ropes, and to assist in the transfer of the Allens back to their home city, not to be mooning after the boss! It was her opportunity to prove how capable she was, and she could hardly do that if she was dissolving into a trembling jelly every time he breathed on her!

'Here's a folder Rose prepared for you before we left.'

Peter's voice interrupted the lecture she was giving herself.

'It has a map of Atlantic City with our hotel, the hospital and the nearest shopping centre marked—all the things Rose considers important!'

Melanie took the plastic folder and opened it quickly, using the movement of her fingers as an excuse not to look at him. The teasing note in his voice was almost too much to bear, as it brought back memories of his patience eight years ago, when he'd tried everything—even teasing—to coax her out of her stubborn sulk.

'You might not believe it after seeing the carrier bag I acquired in Dallas, but I'm not an obsessive shopper,' she told him firmly. If she was proving her worth, she didn't want him thinking her frivolous!

She opened the map and read the little notes pencilled in around the margin before adding, 'But I would like to get something to take home for Kip and my parents, and shopping centres are a good place to see the locals, as distinct from other tourists.'

'I'll see that we sample the best of them,' he promised indulgently.

A slow trickle of something akin to fear started in her blood, cooling her body as it traced through her veins. Jan had told her that staff usually had some time to explore the places they visited, as a two-day turn-around was necessary to ensure that they were fit for the return flight, but she had pictured this exploration as a solo expedition.

How could she handle the silly reactions of her body, if she was constantly in the man's presence? Her ability to maintain the pretence of a calm indifference to him was limited, especially when he was being nice to her!

'I don't know if it's lunch, dinner or breakfast, but we're about to eat again.'

His deep voice broke into her thoughts, and she sighed as he reached across and unlatched her tray from the seat in front of her, his arm resting briefly on her knee in a mimicry of intimacy.

'Anyone would think you hadn't eaten for days,' he remarked a little later as she rested her knife and fork on the tray and poured more soda water in the small plastic tumbler.

'Eating passes the time,' she told him, determined to play the calm, composed international traveller Jan had appointed.

'But it's only one of many pleasurable physical activities to do that,' he said, breaking open his bread roll with his lean fingers, 'although they're not all possible on a plane.'

His voice was soft, yet suggestive, and she fancied

she heard a smile in it. She wanted to look at him, to see if she could read what he felt in his face, to see if she could tell if he was flirting with her.

But he wouldn't do that! He hadn't even wanted to bring her on this trip.

She was well aware that office affairs were possible in any situation, and had seen plenty in her work at hospitals, but Peter Wade did not strike her as a man who would cheat on his wife. For a moment, her concentration on her food lapsed as she followed through her disturbing thoughts.

Could she make that kind of judgement about him? Did she know him well enough? The answer to both questions was no, but. . .

'I'll phone the hospital as soon as we check in and make arrangements for us to see the Allens and the attending doctors this evening if possible.'

She nodded absent-mindedly, her mind still grappling with his behaviour. Surely she would have heard some rumours if he was the kind of man who tried to seduce all the young girls on the staff. Someone would have warned her!

'Once that's taken care of we can rest, and rest includes looking around. It's silly to try and force your body to sleep if it's not ready for it, and best to get into the sleep rythms of this time-zone as soon as possible.'

'Even though we'll be heading back the other way before our bodies have time to adapt?' she asked, deciding it was better to concentrate on her part as the eager young courier than to try to analyse his behaviour and her own erratic responses. 'Perhaps we would be better sleeping during our Australian sleep hours——'

'And partying all night?' he interrupted, with a grin

that would have made her toes curl if she hadn't been being so sensible.

'I suppose it would be a bit hard to expect the American hospital staff to adapt to our time for appointments and such,' she agreed, matching his grin with a wide smile of her own.

The stewardess reached across and removed her tray, hurrying back down the aisle as if they might be approaching an airport, although it was too early for them to have reached Philadelphia.

The 'Fasten Seatbelt' sign blazed as the intercom came to life with a warning to all passengers to return to their seats and fasten their seatbelts as a line of storms was approaching.

The voice had barely died away when the plane plunged downwards with a plummeting, sickening drop that made Melanie regret her hearty meal.

'You OK?' Peter asked, his long, warm hand folding over her fingers, which gripped the armrest so tightly that her knuckles ached.

'It's only a bit of turbulence, Melly,' he added calmly, then let go her hand to slide an arm around her shoulders and draw her close against his chest as the plane lurched and fell again. His free hand prised her fingers loose and then folded around them, drawing them into his lap, while he rubbed the tension away, murmuring soothingly to blot out the cries and gasps of alarm from other passengers and the high, keening wail of a terrified child.

'It'll pull out of it soon,' he assured her as they were thrown against their seatbelts when the plane jolted forward with the unevenness of a car on a badly rutted road. 'These things are built to withstand enormous pressure.'

The cabin tilted, and they seemed to hang, suspended sideways in the air for so long that Melanie heard a thin whimper issue from her lips although she was unaware that she was afraid. Then the shuddering giant straightened itself, and battled on, the fury growing less as it ploughed out of the turbulence.

'You can stop holding your breath now,' Peter whispered in her ear, and she let out the pent-up air in a deep sigh, turning her head slightly. Her parted lips were only inches from his, and her eyes could not avoid the startling blueness of his gaze.

The kiss was inevitable, a celebration of the fact that they were still alive, a mad release of tension that turned from a hearty congratulatory pressing of lips into a thirsting, questing, demanding exploration, reaching deep into Melanie's soul and laying bare all her doubts and denials.

Even as her body responded, moving against his, losing itself in a melting, stirring, joyous release that made her ache with wanting more and more, her mind continued to operate, clattering out disjointed scraps of information and interrogation like an out-of-control machine.

Was it because she had never felt this spark of flame igniting her entire body that none of her friendships with other men had developed into 'relationships'? it asked. She shouldn't be doing this, it reproved. How could he affect her in this way? it demanded, then added the chorus, He's a married man, married man, married man!

'Excuse me, sir!'

Melanie heard the words but could not understand them, then the cough that followed penetrated her brain and she pushed herself away from Peter, turning her flaming face towards the window and peering out as if to find the source of all the turmoil.

'There've been a few minor injuries, and one passenger is in severe pain. You're the only doctor on board and the captain wondered if you would mind having a look at them.'

Peter was out of his seat and following the stewardess down the aisle before Melanie had recovered enough to realise that she might also be useful.

The scene in the back section of the plane was like the aftermath of a disaster as passengers wept, embraced, or cried out, all reacting to the tension in unexpected ways, amid a chaotic jumble of scattered belongings. Cabin staff were attending to those who had suffered minor injuries, and Peter bent over an elderly woman who was leaning forward in an aisle seat, holding her forearm tenderly against her body.

He turned and saw Melanie coming up the aisle and called to her to bring bandages for a sling and swathe from the medicine chest the staff had open on a vacant seat.

'I think there's an anterior dislocation of the head of the humerus. I don't want to try and pop it back in, in case it's due to a fracture,' he told her, moving his fingers around the shoulder girdle of the injured woman. 'Get one of the small pillows from the luggage compartment and put it between her arm and chest then tie a sling, and swathe it to keep the limb immobile. I'll see what the plane carries for pain relief, and be back after I've checked on a child who was burnt by hot tea.'

'I'm Melanie Ashcroft, and I'm a nurse.'

Melanie was pleased when the older woman murmured her name in response. She might be shocked,

but while she could still respond to social conventions
all was well.

'You heard Dr Wade explain that he thinks you've
fractured your collarbone,' she went on, slipping the
pillow into place and sliding the material for the sling
under the injured arm. 'I know it's painful, but it will
hurt less once we get it immobilised.'

She made a pad of a smaller bandage and placed it
on the patient's uninjured shoulder to hold the knot of
the sling, then folded the material and knotted it to
take the weight of the injured arm, with the hand
slightly elevated. She tucked the end around Mrs
Grant's elbow and pinned it in place, before tying the
swathe around her body to immobilise the arm.

She checked the radial pulse and the colour of the
fingertips and was reassured that there were no indi-
cations of a loss of circulation or feeling.

'Can you find a comfortable position to sit back in?'
she asked, and watched the woman ease herself gin-
gerly back in the seat.

'I've some pain-killers in my handbag,' she told
Melanie. 'I take them for migraine. Do you think. . .?'

Her voice was weakening, and Melanie knew it was
pain and shock. She reached for the handbag and
opened it, passing it to the woman who found what she
needed with her free hand.

'I'll check with Dr Wade,' Melanie assured her,
taking the packet so that Peter could read the compo-
sition of the drugs in case the generic names were
different.

'I'll tuck this blanket around you, and be right back,'
she assured her patient, then hurried down the passage
to where Peter was bent over the child.

'They'll be as effective as anything else we could

provide,' Peter told her, squinting at the packet and checking the strength. 'She could take two now, but make a note of what we've done and the time she's taken them for the Airport Medical Service. They will take over when we touch down.'

'Will they land the injured passengers close by or go on to Philadelphia?'

'Fly on, I would think. There are enormous problems involved in diverting a plane.' He smiled at her, adding ruefully, 'It's one of the reasons some companies hate taking our patients—always worried there might be an emergency that will involve them having to land where they're not scheduled to land.'

She smiled back, although her insides were as turbulent as the storm that had tossed the plane around.

'I'll fix Mrs Grant and come back if you need help,' was all she said, and felt proud that she sounded as calm as he did.

The kiss was a reaction, she told herself, moving down the aisle with the tablets and a paper cup filled with water. A reaction she would have to see did not repeat itself. She couldn't fall in love with Peter—he had a wife. What was more, she pointed out to the wayward part of her mind that wanted to argue with this theory, if he was the type of man who cheated on his wife, then he wasn't worth her loving anyway.

'It's all perfectly simple,' she announced, startling Mrs Grant and herself as the words burst out.

'Here,' she told her patient, passing her the tablets and then the little cup. 'I don't suppose you'd have a pen and paper I can use in that handbag?'

The woman nodded, and again Melanie opened it, feeling uneasy as she held it out for Mrs Grant to retrieve what she needed. People's handbags were such personal things!

'I'm writing a note for you to give the medical people at the airport,' she explained. 'It's a safety precaution in case the tablets knock you out and you can't tell them what you've had.'

'So they don't pump me full of something else on top of it, you mean?' the woman asked, and Melanie nodded.

'I'll pin it to the outside of the sling; that way you won't have to worry about losing it,' she explained.

'Well, I must say you're a handy person to have on a plane,' Mrs Grant told her, a trace of colour coming back into her face as the chemicals began to dull her pain.

'It's almost like part of my job,' Melanie told her, smiling broadly as she realised how much she was enjoying working at something that provided such variety, although unexpected variations like the turbulence was something she could live without!

This was definitely the job she wanted to do for as long as possible, she decided. As Kip had said, it was up to her to prove that she was so good, they could not possibly put her off at the end of her trial period.

Calm, composed, unflappable—that was what she had to be.

'Happy about something?'

Peter had joined her in the aisle, his comment wiping the lingering smile off her face.

'I was thinking how much I enjoy this job,' she told him with an underlining nod of her head. 'Is there anyone else who needs attention?'

She'd show him how good she was and ignore all the

stupid distractions that her body and his proximity kept
hurling in her path.

'One of the stewardesses was hit by the heavy food
trolley and jammed against a wall. Fortunately one of
the other cabin staff noticed and secured the trolley
before it went charging back down among the
passengers.'

'And the stewardess?'

'She's resting in First Class—no obvious damage, but
there could be internal problems. I'm going up to see
her now; will you come?'

'Of course,' Melanie replied, and followed him along
the aisle towards the front of the plane.

The woman was pale and sweating slightly, curled
sideways in the wide seat with her knees pulled up as if
protecting a painful area.

Explaining that he wanted to examine her, Peter
eased her over on to her back, and Melanie pushed
pillows under her knees to keep them flexed and ease
the tension on the stomach muscles.

'Where's the worst of the pain?' Peter asked, and
the girl waved her hand vaguely over her abdomen,
but when her gently palpated the left upper quadrant
she flinched away and a greyness seeped into the skin
of her face.

'See if they carry anti-shock trousers,' he said
abruptly, and Melanie turned back towards the medicine chest, only to hear him call after her, 'And get
someone to drop this oxygen mask.'

She hurried away, sending a steward back to provide
oxygen then hesitating over the contents of the medicine chest. Comprehensive it might be, but anti-shock
trousers were not included. She picked up four pieces
of sling material and some wide tape and walked back.

'No luck?'

Peter had his patient wrapped up warmly and was holding the oxygen mask firmly over her face. He looked at the bundle of cloth in her hands and raised an eyebrow.

'I did a first-aid course before I went to Africa,' Melanie said, aware of a slightly defensive note in her voice.

'A trained nurse learning first aid?'

He was smiling as he said it and she smiled back.

'It teaches you different things,' she explained. 'One of them was emergency treatment for closed abdominal wounds where there's a suspicion of internal bleeding. You make a bulky pad and tape it snugly in place over the abdomen. I've no idea why, but I thought you might know and brought these in case you want to try it.'

'Pressure, I suppose. I think it's worth a try. I'm too far out of emergency care to remember clearly. Most of my cases are sitting in hospital and all I have to do is keep the equipment running on the way home.'

She smiled at his self-deprecating words, then watched as he bent over his patient and explained what he was going to do.

'You go back to your seat now, Melanie,' he added, 'I'll stay with Abby until we land.'

Feeling suddenly redundant, she shuffled away, slumping back down into her seat and staring blankly out of the window. Of course Peter had to sit with his patient in case she went into shock, or developed other symptoms. But calling her Abby seemed unnecessarily cosy! Was the man a womaniser? If he didn't have a female staff member to flirt with on his trips, did he use his charm on the stewardesses?

That was something else she'd heard about—the bored businessman whiling away a long flight with a little flirtation, wining and dining a pretty member of the cabin staff at his destination.

Surely Peter wasn't like that!

Philadelphia unfolded beneath her and an excitement she could not control eased through her body, banishing the tiredness and disappointment she had been feeling. It was as if she had been transported into another world, and she started in surprise when a stewardess tapped her on the shoulder.

'Dr Wade wondered if you would collect the baggage and wait by the carousels until he can join you. He'll accompany the injured stewardess through to the medical centre, and our staff will take the injured passengers.'

Melanie nodded. She'd seen the big aluminium carrying case that contained their equipment when Peter had opened it for Customs, and been impressed by the documentation he had handed to the official. Every appliance was listed and described and every drug they carried was noted, to be accounted for on their departure.

This might not be a normal repatriation trip, but, as he had said, it was an opportunity for her to prove herself.

The wheels thumped on to solid ground and the passengers let out an involuntary cheer. Melanie put her bag on the spare seat beside her, then reached up into the locker for Peter's bag, slinging its strap over her shoulder as she waited patiently to disembark.

'Good girl!'

She felt his arm across her shoulder and heard his

voice at the same instant as she stood, leaning slightly on the trolley she'd found, guarding their precious equipment.

'Is Abby OK?' she asked, pleased that she sounded almost normal after a journey that seemed to have lasted for days.

'I think she will be,' he told her, then bent over his luggage, searching through it until he found a folder similar to the one he'd handed Melanie on the plane. Out of it he extracted a large sticker with the UniversAid logo emblazoned on it. He stuck this on the big case and steered the trolley towards the exit, his eyes alert for their driver now that they were easily identifiable.

The man who approached them was short, but gave the impression of wiry strength.

'I'm Matt Carson,' he said, stretching out his hand to Peter. 'I'm with Drive-U and will be your main driver while you're here, although you might get one of the others if I'm off duty.'

Melanie responded to the man's warmth and friendliness with a delighted grin and thrust forward her hand to greet him.

'How far is it to Atlantic City?' she asked, as they emerged into weak late afternoon sunshine and she breathed fresh air for the first time since leaving Brisbane.

'About an hour and a half, depending on the traffic. Pretty quiet this time of the day,' he said, leading the way to a large white limousine parked by the kerb.

'Do we ride around in that thing even when we want to go to the shops?' she asked Peter in an undertone, shocked by the apparent extravagance.

'You'll get used to it,' he replied, smiling at her

egalitarian protest. 'It's the only way to go over here, believe me!'

They watched as Matt loaded their luggage into the boot then Peter opened the rear door of the long vehicle and she slid into an interior that seemed the size of a small living-room.

'Bar there in the middle if you folks want a drink,' Matt told them as he climbed in behind the wheel and set the engine purring.

'I'm disoriented enough without alcohol,' Melanie said in response to Peter's unspoken query.

It's the long trip, she told herself, shutting off her awareness of her companion by looking out of the window. The car slid past suburban streets lined with tall wooden houses, the light traffic flowing smoothly as the day began to draw to a close. She rested her head against the corner cushion and relaxed. They were nearly there!

'I'll drop you off at the hotel and go on to the hospital,' Peter was saying as she came back to consciousness. 'There's nothing to be gained from us both seeing them tonight. You can have a shower and relax for a while. I'll be back in time for us to eat together.'

Was he looking after her because she was new at this business, or was this standard procedure? She wished she knew.

'I'm not that tired,' she protested. 'Why can't we both go to the hospital on our way to the hotel? That way, once we check in we won't have to go out again.'

She must have said the right thing, for his tired face split into a warm smile.

'Are you certain you feel up to it?' he asked. 'It's not standard procedure.' His shoulders moved in a self-derogatory shrug. 'The rule is to get to the hotel and rest before contact, but there's something about this case that's making me feel anxious.'

Melanie felt the camaraderie between them strengthened on this admission and she responded quickly.

'I'm certain I'll rest easier once we've seen them,' she agreed, and Peter leaned forward to tell Matt of their change of plans.

The hospital could have been in any city in Australia, she decided as they swept up the drive to a long, low line of buildings. Well-trimmed flowering shrubs softened the walls, and wide green lawns swept down towards the road.

'You can get the receptionist to call me in the canteen,' Matt told them as they slipped out of the car, Peter pulling on his suit jacket and buttoning one button as they approached the entrance. Melanie tucked her shirt more firmly into her jeans and stood up as tall as she could, hoping she'd pass unnoticed behind Peter.

'Come through this way.'

The soft American accent seemed to lure them forward, and they moved through corridors made more familiar by the distinctive odour that welcomed members of their professions in any part of the world.

'Unfortunately, they're about as far apart as they could be,' their guide explained as they reached the men's surgical ward. 'We have been wheeling Mr Allen over to visit his wife and some of the staff are popping in when they're off duty, but Mrs Allen has been extremely upset, and we haven't really known what to do.'

With her heart beating rapidly now that they were so close to the strangers she thought of as friends, Melanie followed the sister and Peter through to the private

room with its windows looking out over the pretty
garden. Then Peter was introducing himself, and she
was moving forward, to the bedside of a well-built
young man with a shock of dark brown hair.

'Could you go and see Anna?' he begged, anxiety
providing added strength to his handshake. 'She won't
tell me what's wrong, but she's. . .changed, somehow.'

There was bewilderment in the soft brown eyes, and
pain as well.

'I'll leave Dr Wade with you and go right now,' she
assured him. 'If that's OK with you?' she added to
their guide.

'I'll take you over,' the woman said, leading the way
back out of the room and down more corridors, then
into what was obviously the maternity ward.

What a place to put the poor girl! Melanie thought.
The sight of the mothers with their new babies, the
sounds of congratulation, the crying of the new-born
would all exacerbate her own sense of loss.

'Here's a visitor from Australia for you,' her guide
called as she knocked and entered the room without
waiting for a response.

'Mum said you'd come,' the pretty blonde cried,
reaching out to grasp Melanie's hand and squeezing
her fingers until they hurt. 'She rang and said you were
on the way, but I didn't dare believe it. I didn't want
to hope.'

Melanie sank on to the bed, stroking the thin fingers
with her free hand, unable to speak for the big lump in
her throat. She forced herself to swallow, then intro-
duced herself.

'And I'm Anna,' the young woman told her, a
feverish glitter that was more than excitement evident
in her eyes. Melanie's eyes took in the surroundings,

noting the drip that was feeding into Anna's arm. Even before she read the chart, she guessed that infection was present, and, as well as nutrients, the drip was providing a continuous infusion of antibiotics. 'When will you take us home?'

'We've only just arrived but Dr Wade will be speaking to your doctor first thing in the morning,' Melanie explained. 'Once he has all the details about you and your husband, he'll decide what happens next.'

'But he will help us get home?'

'I think so.'

'I'm sure so.'

Mealnie spun around at the sound of the deep English voice, and was surprised to see Peter pushing Mr Allen in a wheelchair through the door.

'This is another Peter,' he explained, with a smile.

'But I'm always called Pete,' the young man hastened to assure her. 'So there'll be no confusion on the way home, will there, honey?'

The unfamiliar American endearment had a pleading intensity, as if all he wanted was for his wife to share this mild joke.

Melanie felt Anna's uninterest as if it were a physical presence in the room, and wondered what had gone so desperately wrong between them at a time when they should be leaning on each other for support.

'I thought it best if we discussed the arrangements together,' Peter broke in, as if he too sensed the tension in the air. 'And I've also told Pete this will be the last ride he gets. I want him practising on his crutches as much as possible.

Melanie nodded. The sooner Pete was mobile, the less chance there was of a thrombosis in his leg. With the inactivity of a long flight ahead, the risk was higher.

'Can we leave tomorrow?' Anna's eagerness would have been amusing if the note of desperation hadn't been crystal-clear in her voice.

'Maybe the next day,' Peter explained from the foot of her bed where he was studying her file.

Melanie felt Anna's grip tighten on her hand and saw the tears that gathered in her eyes. She leaned towards her, hoping to hide the other woman's disappointment, passing on messages from her mother and talking inanely about the weather at home and the long flight from Australia.

'Well, we just dropped in to let you know we're here,' Peter said at last. 'We'd better go now and check in at the hotel before they decide we're not coming. Do you want to stay here with Anna, Pete, or will I take you back to your own room?'

'You'd better go,' his wife answered fretfully, and Melanie saw the disappointment on the young man's face.

'Well, we'll all go together, and Melanie and I will be back to see you in the morning,' Peter said, sounding so cool and detached that Melanie wanted to hit him.

Outside the window, darkness was hiding the gardens, and street-lights were beginning to glow. She felt Anna's hand tighten on hers.

'Can you come back and see me after you've settled into your hotel?' she pleaded, and Melanie had opened her mouth to say yes, when Peter interrupted with a quick,

'This is Melanie's first trip with UniversAid and after thirty hours in the air I think she'll be ready to fall into bed as soon as she's eaten.'

There was something fussily pedantic in his tone,

and Melanie felt herself stiffening. Who was he to decide what she did or didn't do? Training and protocol forbade arguing in front of patients, so she squeezed Anna's hand then bent to kiss her flushed cheek.

'I'll be back as soon as I can,' she whispered to her, and followed Peter and his charge towards the door, glaring at his back to give vent to some of her anger.

'She needs someone with her,' she told him as they strode together down the corridor after settling Pete back into his bed.

'She also needs someone who will be capable of supporting her all the way home, which you won't be if you overdo things tonight,' he told her sharply.

'I'd forgotten how bossy you were,' Melanie muttered, quickening her pace to keep up with his long strides.

'Had you?' he said, casting a glance over his shoulder at her. 'Well, I haven't forgotten how impossible you become when you're overtired. Nothing much has changed, eh, Melly?'

She couldn't tell if he was teasing her, or if the unfamiliar inflection in his voice was reproof.

'I'm not tired,' she muttered ungraciously, then realised that arguing over something utterly pointless undoubtedly indicated exhaustion. But she couldn't let it rest, and, as they came to a halt beside the reception desk, she added with a childish pout, 'And don't call me Melly!' then remembered that she'd intended to be cool, composed and capable.

She could have cried with frustration!

CHAPTER FIVE

THEY were booked into a suite at Bally's Grand Hotel, a place that seemed to Melanie, as she walked through the foyer, to be a huge poker-machine palace.

'Why a suite?' she asked suspiciously as they rode up to their rooms.

'Because we need space. It's possible this journey will have to be done in stages,' Peter explained, impatience straining his voice. 'Contrary to what you might believe, a thirty-hour plane trip is not the ideal convalescence for seriousy injured people.'

'So what do we do?' she asked as they were shown into a lavish sitting-room by the bellboy.

'I don't know, and won't know until I've spoken to the doctors who are caring for them.'

'Some doctors!' she muttered belligerently, ignoring the comfortable furnishings in the room. 'Fancy putting the woman in the maternity section were she's surrounded by reminders of her own loss.'

'It's standard procedure,' he replied with infuriating calm. 'You can hardly expect the consultant gynaecologist to be trailing all over a hospital that size to visit one extra patient.'

'Oh, no! We wouldn't want to upset a doctor, now would we?' she bit back at him as something she could not control forced her to bait him.

'Why not?' he said. 'You never mind doing it!'

The words were so quietly spoken that she might almost have imagined them, but they killed the impulse to fight as effectively as a bucket of water quenched a small fire.

'Your room is through that door,' he added, waving his hand towards the right. 'Maybe a shower will improve your temper.'

A shower wasn't likely to wash away her concern about Anna Allen, but she picked up her belongings and trudged through into a large bedroom complete with two queen-size beds, and a private bathroom opening off it.

This constant bickering with the boss was hardly the way to prove her composure and competence, she reminded herself, shaking out her new suit and hanging it up in the small wardrobe. Vowing to keep her opinions to herself in future, she pulled clean clothes out of her bag and walked through into the bathroom.

Steaming hot water and plenty of soap washed away grime and tetchiness, so that she emerged tired but definitely more relaxed. She shrugged into the thick towelling robe supplied by the hotel and was rubbing her hair dry when she heard Peter's voice.

'Do you want to dress and go down to the dining-room for a meal, or shall we order something to eat up here?'

Walking into the bedroom, she saw his head poked around the door, his bare shoulders, tanned and wide, also visible. Again the word 'intimate' flickered in her mind.

'I'd much rather eat up here,' she said quickly. 'Then I can fall into bed straight after the meal.' The word 'bed' now jolted her, and she added quickly, 'I am tired!' and hoped this admission would serve as an apology for her pre-shower behaviour.

'I'd never have guessed,' he replied with the same

curious smile that had startled her earlier. 'What would you fancy for dinner?'

'Something light,' she said quickly, covering her confusion with words. 'Maybe a hamburger would be the appropriate choice.' She smiled back, but all he did was nod, and disappear like a genie withdrawing into his bottle.

The situation of a man and a woman travelling together was disturbingly domestic, she decided, combing the tangles out of her hair. As she leaned towards the mirror, she noticed how the front of the bathrobe gaped, revealing too much of her full, thrusting breasts.

This is business, she reminded herself, deciding to put on her clean jeans and a T-shirt. There were enough problems in her mind without adding the ridiculous image of the two of them together in matching bathrobes!

He was wearing a pair of navy blue casual trousers and a paler knit shirt that clung to his spare frame like a second skin, defining his pecs and deltoids, not strongly developed as a result of weight-lifting, but firm and hard as if they were put to regular use in more practical pursuits.

'Have you seen the Atlantic yet?'

'The Atlantic Ocean?' She shook her head as if to clear it, realising she had completely forgotten that they were in a foreign country with new sights to see, new streets to explore.

'It's right out there through the windows,' he added, putting a casual arm around her shoulder and drawing her towards the heavily curtained side of the room. Thrusting aside the drapery and sliding open the glass door, he guided her through, his arm dropping away, but his body still so close behind her that she fancied she could feel him breathing.

'It's like a picutre of the place in a travel brochure,' she whispered as her eyes took in the lamplit boardwalk stretching north and south away from the hotel. Beyond that, a cloud-veiled moon cast pale shadows on the moving ocean, whose might, unrecognisable in the restless, silvered sheen of the water, was heard in the dull thunder of the waves tumbling on the shore.

'I'd forgotten we were here,' she added, trying to explain her feelings yet not wanting to break the spell of harmony that had settled on them both.

'It's a good thing to be preoccupied with your patients,' he told her, moving to stand beside her, his hands outstretched to grasp the rail. 'But not to the exclusion of all else,' he continued, 'and especially not at the expense of your own health and well-being.'

He's reminding me that it's a business trip, she realised. Teaching me things I'll need to know if I'm travelling alone!

She shook away a contrary sadness. They were sharing this adventure as co-workers, nothing else, and the sooner she got that through her thick skull the better, she chided herself, turning her back determinedly on the suggestive moonlight-on-water scene and walking back into the brightly lit sitting-room.

'You were right about Anna being in the wrong place at that hospital,' Peter said as they sat down to tackle the enormous hamburgers that Room Service had provided. 'It's always hard on miscarriage patients to be in the O and G ward, but it is where they'll get the best specialist care.'

Melanie nodded, accepting his words as a truce.

'There's something wrong between Anna and Pete,'

she said, pleased to be back on a professional topic. 'The air fairly crackled with static when you wheeled Pete in.'

'And I thought. . .'

Again he spoke so softly that she wondered if she'd heard the words, but a quick glance at his face revealed nothing more than a wry grin.

'I did wonder,' he said now, ignoring the half-finished sentence. 'Pete seemed overly anxious for a man about to go home.'

He picked up a long potato chip in his fingers and Melanie watched as he raised it absent-mindedly to his lips and bit into it with strong white teeth. His lips were soft, a contrast to the hardness, and she found herself licking her own lips, gone suddenly dry.

'Any suggestions?'

The question brought her back to earth.

'Maybe all they need is time together, time to talk and sit in silence, to hold hands and share a physical comforting,' Melanie offered shyly.

'Which they won't get if they go straight home.' He spoke with such emphasis that Melanie wondered if he knew something she didn't know, but his face had a shuttered look that closed her out, and she knew she must learn not to question every statement he made, or argue with every decree.

Finally, he pushed his plate back and looked at her across the table.

'They won't be able to cope without help for a while,' he told her, 'which means they'll have to go to one or other of their parents' homes. Their friends will pop in to hear about the holiday, and commiserate about the accident, and time alone will be the last thing they'll get.'

'But we can't do anything about that,' Melanie argued, forgetting her decision to remain passive. 'They won't be our responsibility then.'

'That doesn't sound like the young woman who wanted to spend the night holding Anna's hand,' he mocked, and all her resolutions flew out the window.

'I'm only trying to remain detached,' she told him haughtily, 'as ordered by my boss! Maybe the solution is to put them in hospital when they get home, until they can manage on their own!'

'The hospital here isn't helping heal whatever rift exists, so why should an Australian hospital?'

The well-being that the hot shower and hearty food had engendered began to drain away. Was this part of her work experience, this needling at her to argue both sides of the case?

'Well?' he demanded.

'Well, what?' she replied crossly. 'I don't see what we can do! Unless we. . .'

She paused, twirling her fork in her fingers, while she ran through the skeleton of an idea in her head, searching for the objections he was sure to make.

'Unless?' he prompted.

She looked up to see his eyes on her face, an eagerness there that she couldn't quite understand.

'Could we bring them here for a day or two before we go? The rooms have two beds so he wouldn't constantly be crashing his cast into her, but they would have time together and we could look after them.'

She saw the smile spread across his face and the gleam of excitement in his eyes.

'You did grow up into a sensible young woman, Melly Ashcroft,' he said, his voice warm with praise. 'And we might make a courier out of you yet! You've got to learn to think on the run. Often we arrive at a place after a horrific journey and find the situation is totally different from our expectations. A courier must be able to adapt, to change plans, routes, medication, whatever!'

The pleasure of his praise swept through her, banishing all other thoughts.

'Is that what we'll do?' she asked, her eyes sparkling with delight that she'd guessed correctly, yet as she watched his face she saw his smile fade and the controlled, mask-like expression slip back into place.

'If you can handle sharing the other bedroom with me,' he said, his voice devoid of all emotion.

Opening her mouth to protest, she remembered his words about thinking things through, and closed it quickly.

The couple would need care. Anna especially would have to be checked during the night. If she remained on the drip, it would have to be monitored. It would be impossible to dump them in a room and have to tiptoe around the hotel corridors at night in order to reach them.

'Worked it out?' She looked up to see Peter's eyes fixed on her face, a slight tightening of his lips making him look grim.

'I think so,' she told him, then remembered her suspicions about his behaviour towards her earlier. 'But surely I could sleep here in the sitting-room.'

She waved a hand towards the small couch.

'There are two extremely large beds in each bedroom, Melanie,' he reminded her. 'And all we'll be doing there is getting enough sleep to make sure we can take the Allens safely home.'

He made it sound as if *she* were the one not to be

trusted, she thought resentfully, then remembered her behaviour in the past and felt the blush sweep upwards.

'Speaking of sleep has made me realise how much I need some,' she mumbled, standing up and heading towards the door of her room. 'What time will we be leaving for the hospital in the morning?'

'We won't be,' he told her. 'You'll stay here and rest while I go over and meet Dr Reynolds. I'll find out what I can, and be back by ten o'clock. The arrangements we make from there on will depend on what he has to say.'

Stifling the urge to demand that she go with him, she nodded her agreement, then said goodnight and departed. Anna would hardly expect her to be visiting at eight o'clock in the morning, and the thought of a good night's sleep was infinitely tempting.

Melanie woke to a sense of loss, a name falling from her lips in the half-conscious state that preceded complete awareness.

In her dream, she'd lain with Peter, his muscled arm heavy across her shoulders, protecting a sleep that had been deepened by a strange satisfaction. Her body stirred, remembering, and she was struck by a peculiar sense of shame and bewilderment.

As her recollections of the dream grew clearer, she twisted uncomfortably. Adolescent boys had sexy dreams; she knew that from her studies. But women?

None of her friends had ever mentioned it, she thought, rubbing her hands over her body as if to satisfy the longings that still twitched beneath her skin.

She sat up, looking around the still dark room, trying to orient her mind and body. The little travelling alarm by the bed told her it was seven o'clock, local time, but she knew her restless body would not allow more sleep.

Slipping out of bed, she crossed to the window and pushed back the curtain, shivering at the cold greyness of the ocean that splashed on to the beach far out beyond the board-walk. Beneath her, joggers and walkers dotted the boards.

She'd go for a run!

Dressing quickly, she pulled on the light windproof jacket over her T-shirt and shorts, laced up her shoes, and left her room through the door that led directly into the hallway.

She found the lobby deserted except for the bellboys, although she could hear music and muted voices from the area beyond the entrance, where gambling tables operated all night. Anxious to breathe fresh air, she headed past the banks of poker machines and out into the cold, crisp morning.

She stretched against the raised edge of a garden bed, then crossed the road, falling in behind two male joggers who chatted quietly as they ran. Their pace was perfect for a warm-up run, she decided, peeling off her jacket and tying it around her waist as her arms and legs began to loosen with the exercise.

Ten minutes later, she pulled out from behind her pacemakers, and stepped up her pace, running easily and breathing deeply. It was exhilarating and a sense of well-being stole over her, banishing the silly stirrings of her body.

Peter Wade was giving her every opportunity to prove herself capable of doing a good job. It was still a probationary period, and she was constantly under review, her behaviour monitored and her decisions checked.

His rare lapses from guide and mentor into something more—friendly?—were not the advances of a man who wanted a bit of fun outside his marriage, but another part of the same test. What kind of courier would she make if she fell into bed with every attractive man she met along the way?

If she'd been more mature, like the people they usually employed, the problem might not have arisen, she decided, running automatically, oblivious of her surroundings as her mind cast around for solutions that would explain Peter's behaviour.

That must be it, she told herself, then accelerated, as if to flee the answers she had found. Her feet pounded on the grey boards, and her chest rose and fell as she breathed in the oxygen she needed to feed her straining muscles.

Now the scene opened up before her and her eyes photographed impressions as she passed. The hotels that had lined the street further back had given way to houses, two or three-storeyed wooden structures, some painted bright colours, others weathered to a grey that matched the dirty ocean.

She turned, determined to take some time later in the day to explore what lay beyond the famous walkway. Now she needed exercise, needed the adrenalin rush her efforts would provide, and the physical exhaustion at the end of it.

There was a sharp rap on the interior door as she slipped back into her room from the hall. Peter must have heard her return, and wanted to give her some last-minute instructions.

She opened it to him, surprising a look of repressed anger on his face.

'Please leave a note if you're going out,' he said stiffly, his eyes sliding over her sweat-sheened arms and down legs that looked longer in the brief, wide-legged running shorts.

'I didn't realise you'd look in on me before you left,' she said, shivering slightly as her body started to cool.

'You might have known I'd want to check,' he snapped, backing away from the door.

Bemused by his behaviour, she remained where she was, watching as he gathered up some papers he must have been studying over breakfast, and shoved them into a slim leather folder. She wished she could see his face, which was bent away from her, although she knew how hard it was to read his mood in that stern visage.

When he finally looked up at her, his mood was not hidden after all, for a frown had drawn his black brows together and slammed his lips closed as tightly as a steel trap.

'Get yourself showered before you catch cold in that skimpy outfit, and I'm not certain that running alone is sensible, particularly in a foreign country,' he said coldly.

He made it sound as if they were in the wilds of Afghanistan!

'There were probably two hundred other people out there running or walking,' she told him sweetly, 'but if you'd like to accompany me tomorrow I'd be happy to have your delightful company.'

She smiled at his scowling face and waggled her fingers in a little wave of farewell. It was all part of the test, she reminded herself as she shut the door with exaggerated caution although her instinct prompted her to slam it in his face. It was a test she intended to pass with flying colours!

The phone rang as she emerged from the shower.

'I'm sending Matt back to the hotel,' Peter's voice informed her, dispensing with polite preliminaries. 'Have your breakfast then hop over here; the problem you mentioned is worse than we feared and I'll need your persuasive tongue.'

Was he being sarcastic?

'Should I meet you somewhere first or go straight to Mrs Allen's room?'

'Straight to her room would be best. I'll see you in an hour.'

The disconnecting click told her the call was over. Business was business. She dressed quickly, deciding to wear the skirt she had brought from Brisbane with a striped T-shirt that matched it perfectly. A little make-up covered the shadows of tiredness that lingered under her eyes, and a few hearty strokes with the hairbrush brought the shine back to her bright hair.

'Efficient, composed and capable,' she told her reflected self, then gathered up her handbag and jacket and left the room.

'Breakfast is being served through here, ma'am,' a smiling bellboy told her in response to her enquiry. He led the way through a wide passage lined with poker machines, and into a long room with scattered tables made private by screens of potted plants. Voices and laughter echoed round the space as Melanie slipped into a chair at a vacant table.

'Coffee?'

A waitress had appeared in front of her with a steaming pot of fresh brew that smelt so delicious, she had to have it, although at home she would have chosen tea.

Ordering breakfast was harder! The menu offered an enormous choice for someone used to cereal and toast, and even after she had decided what to have she had more choices to make. It appeared that American breakfast eggs came in a multitude of ways!

Was the Allens' problem the result of the accident— or could the problem have been partially to blame for the accident? Arguments in cars could lead to less concentration on road and traffic conditions.

Her thoughts detracted from the delicious breakfast as she prepared to face whatever might lie ahead. And why Peter would think that she'd be of help in a marital crisis situation she did not know, she decided, finishing a second cup of coffee. He was the one who was married!

It's part of the job, Melanie, she reminded herself as she left the room and hurried out to the lobby to find Matt.

'I don't want to see Pete at all!' Anna informed her, defiance written all over her pretty face as Melanie came quietly into the room.

'Well, we can't take you home, in that case,' Melanie told her briskly. 'We do a double deal or nothing.'

She felt mean as she watched the fight die out of the anxious eyes, to be replaced by despair.

'I don't mean to sound harsh,' Melanie assured her, hurrying to perch on the edge of the bed and take her hand, 'but you still need a doctor in attendance if we're to fly you home. Dr Wade and I can't possibly split up to take you and Pete on separate planes.'

Ignoring the pout that had appeared as she explained, she hurried on.

'Has Dr Wade explained that we'd like to get you out of here and into the hotel for the night? We're trying to break the trip into stages to make it easier for you.'

'He said something about it, but I don't want to share a room with Pete.'

Hearing this ungrateful reponse, Melanie felt like slapping her patient. There was an obvious solution: she and Anna could share one room while the two Peters had the other.

Anna had begun to list her husband's shortcomings, but Melanie ignored her, trying to decide what would be better for Pete and Anna before blurting out this idea.

'Have these things always bothered you?' she asked, remembering that the couple had been married for years.

'Yes! No-o-o! I don't know! Maybe being away with no one but him for so long made it all worse.'

'Maybe you were overtired with the travelling and your pregnancy. Maybe petty grievances became exaggerated on the trip. Tell me where you've been.'

It was a wise move, for Anna brightened immediately and spoke of the beginning of their holiday with such remembered joy that Melanie knew the dissatisfaction with Pete had not been present throughout the holiday. Slowly, she led her through the places they had visited, the things they had seen, hearing the love the two of them had shared in the memories of this recent past. Then Anna's voice changed as she told of New York. They had spent a week there prior to driving south to the Atlantic coast where disaster had overtaken them.

'What happened in New York, Anna?' she asked gently, recapturing the fluttering hand that had slithered from her grasp. 'Talking about it might help.'

The silence dragged on for so long, she thought she might have failed, then suddenly the story came tumbling out.

'We'd been to the theatre one night and were walking back to our hotel when these young kids grabbed hold of a man in front of us and started pushing him around.'

'Oh, heavens!' Melanie responded faintly, assuming the poor woman had seen a murder committed and would have the haunting memory of it with her forever.

'I wanted to run away, find a policeman or get help or vanish—anything!—but would Pete come with me?' The anger was raising the pitch of her voice, forcing the words through the remembered tension. 'He had to help!' she wailed. 'He handed me his suit jacket and rushed in there to get himself killed, forgetting all about me and the baby.'

Now she was crying in earnest, racking sobs interspersed with little whimpers of distress and helpless sniffles. Melanie put an arm around her shoulders and drew her close, patting at her shoulder and murmuring soothing nothings.

'It was probably an automatic response for him to get involved. No one likes to see a person being attacked. I would think a man's natural impulse would be to help.'

'But he could have been killed,' Anna sobbed, and Melanie knew that everything would be all right if only she could get the two of them back together again.

If Anna's despair had been because she herself might have been killed, then the marriage could well have been beyond repair. Anna felt aggrieved that he'd deserted her, but her real terror had been for him, and somehow the thought of life without Pete remained with her still, curdling her thoughts about him and her feelings towards him.

'Have you told him how worried you were at the time?' she asked, and felt the girl nod against her chest.

'I told him how selfish his actions were,' she mumbled, 'and all he did was argue that he had to help. Then I said, See if I care if you get yourself killed, and after that things got worse and worse then the bus turned out of the lane and hit us and I lost the baby and there's nothing left for me. Not even Pete.'

'You've been through too much emotional strain as well as the physical injury and shock,' Melanie told her. 'Maybe you'll feel differently once you get home, so that has to be our first priority.'

Her feeling that the Allens needed time together was stronger than ever, and she wondered how Peter was getting on with his piece of the problem.

'Dr Wade is determined that you both move to the hotel as soon as he can get your release organised. Once there, you can have a proper rest before we leave. We're trying to arrange a direct flight to Los Angeles to cut down on travelling time. We'll rest again overnight in an airport hotel before tackling the last leg home.'

'As long as I don't have to be in with Pete,' the girl reminded her with a mulish look on her face.

Poor Peter, Melanie thought, remembering her own equally fractious stubbornness when he'd been trying to help her. Then the great idea was born! Thinking of

Peter and their journey together had given her the clue she needed.

Summoning a suitably coy expression to her face, she turned to Anna, beginning hesitantly.

'Well, if you really couldn't bear to share with him, I suppose we could swap, but it's very awkward, you see. . .'

The sentence stumbled so convincingly that she knew she had caught Anna's attention.

'It's like this. . .' Again she paused, hoping the shame she felt at the lie was causing a becoming blush. 'You see, Peter—that's Dr Wade—and I are just married——' she had slipped an African ring from one hand to the other as she'd thought of the idea '—and we were supposed to be on our honeymoon when this trip came up, and we've been on planes for what seems like days and days, and last night I was so tired. . .'

Again she let her voice trail off, but the stiffening of Anna's shoulders told her she'd broken through the self-pity that had been blocking her thoughts.

Then the blush that she had practically forced into place turned to a burning chagrin as she felt a hand settle on her shoulder and knew immediately that Peter was in the room behind her.

At what stage of her story had he slipped silently into the act? There was no time to wonder, although she could feel her body beginning to tremble beneath his touch. Anna was speaking, her words rushing out as she turned from the assured to the assurer.

'Well, I suppose Pete and I can put up with a night together for a good cause,' she conceded with the kind of roguish smile people bestowed on newly-weds. 'It must have been dreadful to have your honeymoon disrupted this way. Why, Pete and I——'

She stopped abruptly, but the thought must have continued in her mind, for a sweet smile spread across her face and the defensive control softened before their eyes.

'When do we leave?' she asked Peter, while Melanie squirmed under his firm grip, wishing to distance herself from his touch and the insidious messages of his body.

'I should have you all signed out in an hour,' he promised her. 'Melanie can take the car and collect your personal belongings that are being held at the hotel where you'd been staying.'

'It will be good to get into some of my own clothes,' Anna told him with a beaming smile. 'And to be able to get around without the drip-stand.'

'We might have to keep the drip for a while,' Peter warned her. 'I haven't seen your specialist yet, which means I don't know if he'll insist on intravenous antibiotics, or agree to change you on to oral medication.'

'But I'm feeling much better,' Anna argued, then the corners of her mouth drooped and she added a pitiful, 'Physically, anyway!'

'The pain of loss takes longer,' Peter said quietly, then bent and whispered to Melanie, 'Would you please wait outside for a few minutes?'

It was such a formal request that she knew she was in trouble. Telling Anna that she and Peter were married had been stupid, but she'd been unable to think of any other excuse to get the couple into the same room.

The few minutes stretched to fifteen, and she wondered what Peter was finding to talk about, while her own agitation grew and grew, fed by the imaginary conversations with him that she was practising in her mind.

By the time he emerged, pulling the door closed behind him, she was so overwrought that she met the expected reproof with an excuse before he had time to speak.

'You told the same lie to get us into that hotel in Lisbon. I know they need to be together, and it was the first thing that came into my head.' She glared at him as she spoke, daring him to argue.

'It's OK Melly,' he replied, not smiling, but not frowning either. 'Now, here's the address of the Allens' hotel, a note from Pete authorising you to collect their things, and a signed traveller's cheque to settle their account. Matt will take you there, then back to the hotel, where you'd better shift your gear into my bedroom if you want your story to stick.'

I must look like a flashing neon sign, Melanie thought as the heat swept up into her face again. Calm yourself, she ordered hastily, then lifted her eyes to meet Peter's for the first time since they'd met in the hospital room.

'Do you want me to come back here when I've done that, to help with the transfers?' If he could pretend nothing had happened and concentrate on business, then so could she!

'I think not,' he said. 'Although you could go through their cases and send Matt back to the hospital with clothes for each of them.'

Melanie nodded, pleased to see that he was looking and sounding satisfied with the arrangements.

Then he reached out and touched her again, deliberately, with one finger under her chin, tilting it up towards him so that her eyes could not avoid his. Her body filled with fire.

'It's going to mean you won't have much time for shopping, sightseeing and exploring, bringing the Allens out of hospital like this. One of us will have to be with them all the time, you know, and the other should be resting or sleeping. I'm sorry to spoil your trip this way.'

'As if I care about that,' she said stoutly. 'We're here to do a job, aren't we? Not to be tripping about the neighbourhood.'

'You *have* grown up,' he said, leaning towards her to murmur the words in a peculiarly husky undertone, while his eyes held hers with an intensity that made her shiver. 'Grown up in many different ways.'

Then he bent as if to drop a kiss on her parted lips and she found herself holding her breath as she waited, but he jerked upright suddenly, and his hand fell away, brushing against her neck and skimming oh, so lightly against one taut breast.

CHAPTER SIX

MELANIE turned and fled. It was sexual harassment, that was what it was! And in a hospital corridor of all places.

She found Matt in the hospital lobby and gave him the name of the Allens' hotel while her mind juggled with a dozen different concerns. Anna's problem won, and she wondered if sharing a bedroom for a day and a night would help her and Pete sort out their problem.

On the other hand, her and Peter's sharing a bedroom was likely to exacerbate her own confusion, as the tug of physical attraction she already felt for him was likely to be strengthened by the close proximity.

'What is this place?' she demanded of Matt as he pulled into the drive of a huge, ornate, painted palace.

'It's the Taj Mahal, ma'am,' he told her, his voice apologetic as if he, a local, felt some collective responsibility for the ostentatious décor.

'It's certainly different,' Melanie told him as she slid out of the car with Pete's cheque and letter of authority. 'I should only be a few minutes.'

The Taj might look like something out of a movie set, but inside the calm American efficiency she had found at the hospital made light of her task. With a vague feeling of distaste at opening someone else's luggage, she found underwear, baggy shorts, shirt and a warm jacket for Pete and a skirt, blouse and cardigan for Anna. She folded these into a small bag, and put it into the car as the heavy cases were loaded into the boot. Matt dropped her and the cases back at the Grand, leaving her with one of the helpful bellboys, while he headed back to the hospital with the small bag of clothes.

Her bed had been made up while she was away, and her room was spotless. It took her a few minutes to gather up her belongings and transfer them to Peter's room, although her hand shook slightly as she hung her suit in the wardrobe beside his neat business shirts.

It's a hotel room like any other, she told herself crossly as the jittery feeling spread through her body. And with separate beds, each the size of a football field, there'll be no accidental intimate moments!

In Lisbon they'd shared a small double bed, fully clothed, but together because he hadn't trusted her not to flee if left on her own. She'd turned to him, half asleep, and, clinging to his shoulders, had sobbed out all the doubts and anguish of the past months in a senseless litany of shame and despair.

He'd held her against his chest, stroking her painfully thin shoulders and murmuring soft, meaningless words into her hair until the racking sobs subsided, and she'd cuddled, like a child exhausted by a tantrum, against him.

When the embrace had changed she could not remember, knowing only that it had. One moment she had been a child and the next an awareness of him as a man had sung through her veins like a wild, tumultuous chorus of desire, firing the nerve-endings that Eduardo had coaxed into sensitivity, and setting her body trembling with a need she had not fully comprehended.

By some osmosis beyond rational explanation, his body had felt and recognised the signals hers was transmitting, and in her mind the carer had become a lover and she had moved against him, unconsciously using her body to tempt his further towards a culmination she had only once experienced and still barely understood.

Here, with her hand on his shirt, and the male smell of him in her nostrils, she remembered the desire that had flared between them, the hot, panting breaths, the twisting, seeking hands, the softness of her body against his hardness, and the silken feel of skin sliding against skin as the barrier of their clothes had disappeared as if by magic.

Hot, slick kisses had pressed against her lips, her throat, her shoulder, and finally her breast, torturing her to an agony of wanting, as she'd twisted in his arms begging for him to relieve the pain, to take away the hunger—to love her, love her, love her!

Had it been the sound of her voice, or the articulation of her need, that had frozen his body so suddenly that she could still remember feeling the heat leave it? He'd turned his back on her, pulling at his clothes, and had climbed from the bed like an old man.

'I have just betrayed everything I believe in,' he had said in a voice so filled with pain that she had cried for him, although he had thought the tears were for herself, had read them as the selfish tears of a spoiled brat who had not been given what she wanted—begged for, in fact!

The jangling summons of the phone brought her back to the present. No wonder he hadn't wanted her working in his company—or accompanying him on this trip! And if she was thinking his behaviour verged on sexual harassment, there must be stronger words for her own provocation eight years ago.

'Could you meet us in the lobby?' Peter asked

quietly, unaware of the turbulent memories his business shirt had dredged up.

Pete was on crutches, the weight of his broken leg supported on a metal frame protruding from the bottom of the cast. Beside him, Anna looked interestingly pale, and alarmingly fragile, as she perched on the arm of one of the big leather chairs that dotted the lobby.

'You should be in a wheelchair,' Melanie told her as she waited with the pair while Peter completed check-in formalities for them.

'I didn't want to be wheeled into a hotel,' she explained. 'I'll put up with it at the airport, but not here.'

'You've only got to get from here to the lift, and then from the lift to our room,' Pete reassured her, although his eyes were anxious as they rested on her white face.

'And you got rid of the drip,' Melanie remarked, wanting to keep the light conversation going.

'Not quite,' Anna told her, raising her left arm so that Melanie could see the IV lock on the catheter in her arm. 'I'll be plugged in again when we get upstairs,' she explained. 'Dr Wade has the solution and antibiotics in his kit.'

Peter walked towards them and Melanie reached out to help Anna up, and took her arm as they walked to the lift.

'Please make use of this sitting-room,' Peter told them as they entered the suite. 'You've been cooped up long enough in the hospital and probably won't want to spend all day in your bedroom.'

He pushed open the door into their bedroom as he

was speaking, and smiled his approval when he saw their cases neatly stacked on the low luggage bench.

'Have a rest for a while, then later you can sort out what you'll need on the journey home, remembering that we'll be stopping for another night in Los Angeles. If you can reduce what you want with you to the small carry-on bags, we'll check the heavy luggage right through to Melbourne.'

Anna nodded, and Melanie wondered if she was the organiser for the couple. She led Pete into the bedroom.

'We'll give you some time to settle in while Melanie and I check up on what we'll need on the flights.' Peter closed the door on the two of them then signalled to Melanie to follow him through into the other bedroom.

'Does she still need IV medication?' Melanie asked, her anxiety about her patient overcoming all other considerations.

'Not really,' Peter replied, 'but she's been on IV fluids since the accident, and as she's still got some bleeding following the miscarriage I thought it best to keep the IV catheter in place. It's only a few days since the accident and major fluid imbalances could still occur.'

'As they would in abdominal surgery?' Melanie asked, thinking through the implications of his words.

'Exactly!'

'So how will you know and what will you do?'

Making rational medical decisions that would have to be carried out on a lengthy plane journey seemed unreal to her.

'I'm going to hook Anna up to a drip whenever we get a chance. Bear in mind that the airlines here won't transport a patient on a drip, and you'll understand that the stop-over in Los Angeles is for more than a good night's sleep.'

'Hook her up overnight, then plug the catheter until we reach the next stop-over.' Melanie shook her head in wonder at the simplicity of the solution. 'What will you give her?'

'She was on whole blood, then lactated Ringer's solution for acute blood loss replacement, but I think we could switch to a slow infusion of five per cent dextrose solution. At 125 ml an hour a 10-gtt-a-millilitre tube will supply the litre in eight hours. If we start now, she can have a night without the drip tubes hooked up, and should be able to sleep better. The dextrose solution should keep her plasma volume stable, and as she's eating normally we shouldn't have a problem with an electrolyte imbalance or a lack of nutrition.'

Melanie nodded, mentally listing the signs of fluid excess or depletion she must watch for when she checked her patient while Peter opened the big case they'd brought with them and pulled out the equipment they would need.

'These bits join up to make a drip-stand,' he told her, handing her some slim metal rods.

And he expects me to know precisely how, she thought, trying to banish the feeling that the accidental touch of his fingers had ignited in her skin.

It was surprisingly easy, she discovered, although she had the advantage of knowing what the end result would look like.

'Do you think Pete's OK?' she asked, as much to break the silence as for any medical reason.

'I think he's fine. They did a scan and could see no internal damage. Anxiety and fear can often produce surprisingly realistic symptoms. I think he was blaming himself for the accident although the police have assured him he couldn't have avoided it.

'Poor man!' Melanie said quietly, setting a sealed IV kit beside the stand. 'He's lost his unborn child as well. I sometimes think the grief of the father-to-be gets forgotten in these tragedies.'

'Little miss soft-heart,' Peter teased as he gathered up the gear they had assembled and headed out of the room to find his patient and hook her up to the drip.

It turned into an enjoyable day as they relaxed in front of the television, marvelling at the choice available to the local viewers and recognising many of the programmes from home. Pete and Anna joined them for lunch, withdrawing to their room for a rest afterwards before joining them again later in the afternoon.

'This is the life, eh, Anna?' Pete remarked as they sat around the table enjoying an unorthodox feast ordered through Room Service. They had each chosen one main meal and one sweet off the menu, and were sharing the dishes in order to try more of what the hotel kitchens had to offer.

It was evidently the opening that Peter had been waiting for.

'So you didn't stay in a hotel like the Taj Mahal every night of your trip?' he asked.

'No way,' Anna told him. 'More often than not it was a youth hostel. We'd saved the Taj for last,' she said, the sadness engendered by the abrupt end to their holiday clear in her voice.

'And then we only had half a night there,' Pete added. 'We arrived late, then left early the next morning to explore the surrounding area, intending to return by lunchtime to really enjoy the hotel facilities.'

'You might come back one day,' Melanie suggested, while Peter diverted Anna with a question about places they had visited on their trip.

The conversation took off, with the pair vying to provide the best insights and the funniest travel stories, the words tumbling so naturally from their lips that before long they were turning to each other for confirmation and smiling at each other as they shared the special memories.

'Early night for all,' Peter said finally, when he detached the drip from Anna's arm at eight o'clock. 'I've arranged wake-up calls at seven, in case we all sleep in. If you wake during the night and need anything at all, press 2 on your bedside phone to make our phone ring. One of us will be in to help you immediately.'

'How much time will we have in the morning?' Melanie asked, not knowing what arrangements Peter had made for the trip home.

'We'll have breakfast at eight and leave by nine. We're driving up to JFK Airport at New York and will fly out from there on Qantas direct to Los Angeles. Overnight accommodation has been arranged at the airport Sheraton, in a suite like this with direct phone contact between our bedrooms.'

'You go to a lot of trouble to make it easy for us,' Pete said, a huskiness in his voice that made Anna turn and take his hand while she nodded her agreement.

Melanie blinked back a tear. They would be all right now, she was certain, but her own reaction worried her. She'd seen people in love before today! So why was their shared feeling causing her to feel misty-eyed?

Maybe it was related to the queasy feeling that had surged through her when Peter had said 'our bedrooms', as if the charade was going to accompany them home.

'Is there anything you need, anything you'd like me to get for you?' she asked Anna while Peter helped Pete through to their bedroom.

'No, thanks,' Anna replied, a slight flush of excitement still colouring her pale lips and shining in her eyes. 'We might be crocks at the moment, but I'm sure we'll manage between us.'

Melanie turned away, but heard Peter speak to Anna as he left the room telling her to keep an eye on Pete and make sure he didn't try to get around without at least one crutch.

'And he'll need some help getting undressed and bathed tonight—and dressed in the morning,' he added, then closed the door, trusting Anna's instincts to take over the role of carer.

'Do you think they'll manage?' Melanie asked doubtfully, following him through to their bedroom. Was Anna ready to do much to help?

'I think so!' Peter replied, flopping down on to one of the beds and stretching his arms above his head, lying spread-eagled and seemingly relaxed against the rich red brocade of the bedspread. 'They'll certainly do better than they were doing in the hospital, even if they have to yell at each other to clear the air. All their feelings were stifled in that artificial world, and their physical injuries made matters worse.'

Melanie nodded, uncomfortably aware that she was hovering in the room, uncertain what to do next, and discomfited by Peter's carefree attitude.

'Well, are you going to stand there all night? Would you like to have a shower and go to bed? Or, if you'd rather, I could get Matt to take you on a tour of

Atlantic City by night. I know the shopping malls will still be open if you want to spend some money.'

She remembered how excited she'd felt at the thought of seeing the city with Peter. Somehow, the prospect of undertaking her exploratory tour with Matt, nice though he was, lacked appeal.

'I think I'll opt for a long, hot shower and then bed,' she said, and picked up her small bag to find her toilet articles and the skimpy pyjamas she'd thrown in when she'd packed, knowing that the hotels would all be heated beyond her comfort level.

Thankful that the hotel provided towelling robes, she hurried into the bathroom. He was gone when she returned to the bedroom, but the light shone from the adjoining room and she noticed that he had shifted the medical case from the bedroom floor. He must be sorting out what they would need on the trip home, she decided, thankful that she had the room to herself.

Leaving the robe on the end of the bed, she slipped beween the sheets, and felt the tiredness she'd been holding at bay steal through her body. The book she'd intended reading remained unopened, and she turned off her bedside lamp and was asleep within seconds.

Peter shook her awake, his hand warm on the bare skin of her shoulder, his voice deep and still husky with sleep.

'Time to move, Melanie,' he said as she struggled back to consciousness. 'Shower's free.'

Prising her eyes open, she sat up in the bed and pushed her hair back from her face.

Peter had turned away, and was buttoning the grey striped shirt that hung out over his dark trousers. His feet were bare, making him seem strangely defenceless.

They were nice feet, long and white, with the boniness she always noticed in his hands. Vulnerable feet, somehow!

'Up now!' the feet's owner said firmly, glancing quickly over his shoulder at her somnolent form. 'I've let you sleep an extra half an hour and Anna may need some help or moral support before she's ready to face breakfast.'

His words shamed her, and she shot out of bed and into the bathroom, pausing only to lift the robe from the foot of the bed and drape it round her shoulders. Not that there was any call for modesty! Apart from his occasional lapses, which she still imagined might be part of some testing process, Peter treated her like a fellow professional—entirely sexless!

'And I'm not disappointed,' she told her mirror self aloud as she stepped under the steaming water.

The bedroom was empty when she returned, and she pulled out her new suit. She was going to New York for the first time, and even if that visit would be a drive through or around the city to the international airport she intended to dress for the day.

Packing the bright blouse that she'd bought with the suit, she pulled out her own gold T-shirt and pulled it on with the skirt. It looked great, she decided, setting the jacket aside to complete the outfit later and packing her belongings swiftly.

Slipping moisturiser and lipstick into her handbag, and checking that her passport and wallet were handy, she set her belongings neatly on the end of her bed, ready to pick up when they were ready to leave. Peter's things were in a similar pile on his bed. Compulsively neat or simply experienced in quick getaways? she wondered.

'Breakfast is here!'

His call reminded her that this was another working day, and she hurried through to the sitting-room to find Anna and Pete already seated at the table. Their clean clothes and relaxed, smiling faces told her that they were managing to look after each other, and had found the love that shock had masked.

'Good morning, you two,' she said, smiling at their contagious well-being. 'Are you ready for your ordeal by flight?'

'It won't be such an ordeal,' Pete told her, his hand reaching out to cover Anna's where it lay on the table. 'More an adventure! Imagine the challenge of pushing your way through airport queues with this,' he added, tapping his cast.

'And every minute in the plane will be bringing us closer to home,' Anna told her.

The smile might be fixed firmly in place but there was a transparency about Anna's skin that worried Melanie. She was pleased when the couple finished their meal and went back into their bedroom to pack, refusing her offer of help.

'Do you think Anna's fit enough for this?' she asked as soon as the door closed behind them.

'Not really.'

Peter's reply surprised her but she waited for him to enlarge on it, knowing now his habit of pausing as if sorting out the most precise words to convey his thoughts.

'But I don't think she was going to get any better in hospital the way things were between them.'

'So if you had your way you'd pop her back in until she's stronger, now that they've sorted out the emotional hassles.'

He smiled at her and her silly heart flipped over.

'We've no time to be debating options, and we don't know how much the thought of going home—right now—contributed to the reconciliation. We have to make our decisions and see them through, but always be prepared for the worst.'

'And what worst should we be prepared for?' Melanie asked, her mind now firmly focused on the professional aspect of the journey ahead of them.

'The worst scenario would be a deep-vein thrombosis in Pete's case, and a haemorrhage in Anna's. Now let's get the medical case unlocked and see what we'll need for either of those possible emergencies, then re-pack them into the smaller case to carry with us on the plane.'

'Interesting case when you consider we've got to carry an anticoagulant for one patient and a coagulant for the other. Should Pete be on a low-dose heparin to prevent clotting? It will be hard for him to move about much in the plane and it's a long flight.'

Melanie stacked absorbent pads into the carry-on case as she spoke, letting Peter go through the drugs they carried to decide what would be needed.

'I spoke to the doctor who's been treating him, and he feels certain he's not at risk. He's a young, fit, healthy man with no predisposition to thromboembolic disease. If you think how long they used to keep patients immobile after surgery, the risk factor for Pete is extremely low.'

'And what of Anna?'

'We'll carry Premarin as a 25mg intravenous injection for an emergency, I'd like you to speak to her before we leave and warn her, without frightening her if possible, that it's a possibility but not something to panic about.'

Peter looked up at her as he spoke, impressing on Melanie the gravity of the situation with a set face and concerned blue eyes. For the first time she realised that UniversAid personnel would often have to weigh up risks and consequences as they took decisions for the people whose well-being was in their hands.

'You'll have to accompany her to the bathroom on the trip, so you'll be able to keep an eye on things,' he continued in the same serious tone. 'As long as she understands to speak up if she feels any discomfort or if there are any changes in her blood loss we should be all right. It's the people who don't want to make a fuss who cause most problems. They are anxious to get home, and because they don't want any hitches they tend to hide symptoms we should know about, often with disastrous results.'

The words were a warning, and Melanie made a silent vow to win the confidence of the people she would travel with, and to impress on them the import-ance of talking about how they felt—all the time if necessary!

'We're packed and ready to leave,' Pete announced, wandering into the room as Peter finished transferring the drugs he would want to the small case.

'I'll have a quick word with Anna,' she told him, and slipped into the second bedroom where Anna rested on the edge of the bed.

'Are you OK?' she asked, and was rewarded with a warm smile.

'Everything's fine,' she said, 'but I still feel so tired. I'm wondering if there might be something else wrong with me.'

'You've lost a lot of blood, and had physical bruises and injuries to contend with as well as worry over Pete and the loss of your baby. It will take a long while for you to pick up, and you've got to make sure you give yourself the time to do it.'

'I can do that once I get home. I gave up my job before we left, although Pete only took accumulated holidays. I'd thought. . .'

'I know,' Melanie told her, hurrying to put an arm around her shoulders and draw her close. 'You'll have another baby, Anna, I know you will but it's important to make sure you're strong and well before you conceive again.'

Sitting down beside her, Melanie explained as carefully as she could about the possibility of haemorrhage, assuring her that it could be treated but it was important not to ignore any early warning signs.

She felt Anna shiver, then the woman's body straightened, and Melanie knew that she would be all right. There was a determined, fighting spirit beneath the young woman's fragility.

With all the precautions taken, the trip was uneventful. They were met at JFK Airport by attendants from the medical centre, who provided wheelchair transport to the two protesting patients and facilitated their transfer to the plane.

'No upgrades, but extra seats,' Peter explained to Melanie when she saw the arrangements that had been made to accomodate Pete's cast. The four of them took up two rows of three seats, with the back removed from one to enable him to rest his foot on the seat in front.

'By sitting in the middle seat, you can shift your foot

to the floor in front of the aisle seat when you get cramped with it straight out in front,' Peter explained as he pushed Pete's crutches under the seat, and propped his leg on a cushion.

Anna took the window-seat and clung to Pete's hand, the excitement and trepidation that warred within her evident in her flushed face and over-bright eyes. Peter and Melanie settled in front of them, one on either side of the cast, a positioning that pleased Melanie, as she did not want to be distracted by the masculinity that her boss's body seem unconsciously to exude.

'So far so good,' Peter remarked, adjusting his seatbelt as the plane taxied towards take-off. 'It's your shift now,' he added, then closed his eyes and appeared to go straight to sleep.

And I might as well have been wearing my old jeans, for all he noticed, Melanie thought, then shuddered at the implications behind that thought. She looked across at his relaxed figure, slumped in the wide seat.

Had he been up to their charges during the night? she wondered, pulling a book out of her handbag to keep her mind off the man and his behaviour. She would be the carer for the patients on this section of their homeward journey. Looking around, she located the bathrooms only a few yards in front of them, then turned and checked through the gap above Pete's foot that her patients were belted in.

Anna's head rested on Pete's shoulder, and she, like Peter, seemed to have drifted off to sleep. Pete nodded and smiled, and she turned back, peering out of the window beyond Peter's profile at the distorted glimpses of the huge city the rising plane had to offer.

So that's New York, she thought, but did not regret not having had time for sightseeing. She was only beginning to learn the intricacies and challenges of this job she had taken on, and was content to concentrate on it to the exclusion of all else.

Well, not quite all else, she admitted silently, stealing a glance at the man who slept only two feet away from her.

Maybe it was a mistake to get too involved in this job. If this silly infatuation she seemed to feel for Peter didn't go away, could she continue to work for UniversAid? Would her own irrational reaction to this man she barely knew mean that she'd have to be the one to make the decision? Would she have to say no, when and if a permanent position was offered in another few weeks?

It was a question that stayed with her through the night in Los Angeles, exaggerated by the fact that sleep would not come, and she was achingly aware of the quiet breathing in the bed beside hers, and of the soft prowling in the night as he checked on their charges.

At times it seemed as if invisible threads joined her body to his, so that she knew every breath he took, every movement he made.

He is not for you, her brain kept telling her, but the messages failed to reach her nerve-endings, which fired continuously, responding to his presence with an errant will of their own.

Could she continue to work with him? The question hovered in her mind as she played her part of the perfect carer all the long, weary way home.

CHAPTER SEVEN

'WELL, how do you feel after your first mission?' Peter asked as they took their seats on the domestic flight in Melbourne. In two hours they would be back in Brisbane, and Melanie was thinking of a hot bath and her own bed when Peter broke the easy silence that had settled between them.

'Tired,' she told him. Not to mention unsettled, cranky and depressed, she could have added but didn't, saying instead, 'I can't seem to feel any particular satisfaction at getting them safely home. I should be glad but. . .'

'You'll feel the satisfaction later,' he assured her. 'Leaving our clients, even with friends and family to support them, is always a bit of a wrench, both personally and professionally.'

'I suppose that's how I feel,' Melanie responded, glad to talk about the safer aspect of her underlying sense of loss. 'It's as if I've abandoned my patients and lost two good friends at the same time.'

She felt him shift in the comfortable airline seat, and even in her exhausted state her body reacted to his movement, traitorously wanting to slide sideways so that her shoulder could brush, accidentally, against his, and feel his warmth. Folding her arms across her chest to avoid contact with him, she stared out of the window, concentrating on what he was saying in order to blot out her own confusion.

For nearly a week Peter had been by her side, and

although he had shown nothing more than comradely interest in her—apart from one tension-filled kiss that didn't count and a few fleeting instances of flirtatiousness!—the thought of parting from him when they arrived home was filling her with an irrational dismay.

'It's a peculiarly close relationship,' he went on, 'this one that develops between couriers and patients. You are together twenty-four hours a day for however long it takes to get the patient home—and in some cases, where the patient is extremely fragile, or the rescue situation remote, this could take up to a fortnight.'

Had he felt like this about her? Had he been reluctant to leave her when they'd finally arrived on the Gold Coast, in spite of her wayward behaviour?

She couldn't ask! Better to keep to the strictly professional aspect of their relationship and hope that their paths wouldn't cross too often at that!

'In another few days,' he added, speaking quietly and calmly as if he sensed her disorientation and wanted to help her through the maze, 'it will be eaier to look back and put it into perspective as a job well done.'

'I hope so,' she told him, aware that she should make some contribution to this conversation, while her mind devised ways she could avoid seeing him at the office. Permanent night duty might be one answer.

'You will,' he assured her, turning to smile at her glum face and pat her gently on the shoulder—a distinctly fatherly as opposed to lover-like gesture! 'You're tired now, and probably jet-lagged as well. After a trip like this, you're due three days off. Phone Jan in a day or two for your new roster hours. She'll also make a time for a debriefing.'

'Debriefing? You make it sound as if it has been a military operation.'

'It's akin to one, Melanie,' he said seriously. 'Although that's just a fancy name we use for sitting down with one of the senior staff and running through the whole scenario. It helps by identifying hitches that can be ironed out in future repatriations and isolating good ideas to be incorporated into future plans.'

'But surely you can do that. You were in charge; all I did was tag along and do as I was told,' she said aloud, aware that she sounded grouchy. She wanted to avoid him, not spend cosy hours in Jan's office reliving their journey together!

Again he smiled, irritating her with his imperturbable good humour in the face of her crankiness.

'We'll each remember different things,' he explained. 'And you'll find it works in your favour as well, because talking it through puts the whole operation into perspective, and Anna and Pete will become nice people you've helped, not friends and patients to be constantly worrying about. We usually conclude with a medical report from the doctor here in Australia on their current state of health, and that ties up the loose ends and closes the case satisfactorily.'

Does it, Dr Wade? she asked silently, turning away from him to look down at the dark green of the tree-clad mountains as they followed the curving ridge of the Great Divide back towards home.

Brisbane spread beneath them, the red roofs like 'Welcome Home' banners strung out especially for her. Her heart lifted and she smiled as she turned to Peter to point out the high, curving arc of the Gateway Bridge spanning the river as it widened on its journey to Moreton Bay.

'Coming home is always special,' he said, smiling back at her, his blue eyes full of warm complicity.

'Is it home for you now?' she asked, as a hunger for more knowledge of this man stirred dangerously within her.

'It has been for a long time, Melanie,' he replied, still holding her gaze, as if his eyes were trying to convey something that his lips could not say.

Home for him and Cynthia! That's what he's saying, she thought, but even that depressing conclusion could not kill the dangerous sense of rapport that his smile had established between them.

The plane touched down, engines roaring as it decelerated across the tarmac. It was impossible to speak—even if there had been words to say. It's just a job that brings people close. He's your boss, and he's married! she reminded herself, watching him stretch his long legs and shrug the stiffness out of his broad shoulders.

They waited until the intial rush for the doors had eased, then Peter stood up and pulled their bags out of the overhead lockers. Slinging them both across his shoulder, he reached down to take her arm, steadying her as she clambered awkwardly out of her seat.

'You've done well, Melanie,' he said quietly, his eyes again holding hers as if to emphasise his words.

Discomfited by his praise, and his closeness, she pushed ahead of him down the aisle. So she *was* being tested all the time they were away! The confirmation of her own suspicions irritated her, although common sense should have told her this would be the case. How else would they know she could be trusted to carry out operations on her own?

'I've got to collect the medical baggage, but then I'll drop you home,' he explained as they walked down the tunnel towards the arrival lounge.

'I can get a cab,' she protested, not wanting to spend any more time with him while she was tired, confused and vulnerable.

'It's on my way, Melly,' he said reverting to the irritating, childish diminutive of her name as he invariably did when she was arguing with him.

'Hi, Melanie!' another voice called, and she looked around the cluster of people waiting in the lounge, to see Barry's beaming face.

'We rang your office to find out when you'd be home. Kip's working so she asked me to meet you,' he explained, greeting Peter like a long-lost friend and bouncing around the two returning travellers like a large and friendly dog.

'Here's Melanie's bag!' Peter handed him the small bag, and turned to Melanie. 'Ring Jan for your duty hours and I'll see you in a few days.'

Then he was gone, striding through the crowd, his shoulders weaving as he avoided the dawdlers, the back of his head as uncommunicative as a fence post.

'Is this all your luggage? The car's out here.'

At least Barry didn't need any responses! He was happy to talk, and rarely waited for an answer to a question before offering a comment or asking something else.

'Thank you for coming,' she said at last as the car headed towards home. The words were not as warm as she'd intended, but that was tiredness. She was so immensely grateful he had come that even the possible repercussions of a renewed interest in her would be worth suffering, as it had saved her from the final effort of pretence with Peter.

* * *

'Can I see you in my office, Melanie?' Jan called from the door of the operations room.

It was Wednesday, and close to the end of her shift, on this, her fourth day back at work. She'd been allocated the early morning time-slot that began at five and finished at midday. The timing had pleased her, as it meant she did not have to see Peter when she came in, and could leave with the other girls on the shift, hiding among them as she walked past his office.

Now she was summoned to Jan's office! It must be for the debriefing he had mentioned the day they returned, and her unruly heart would be put to the test.

He wasn't in the room when she entered and she was steeling herself for his arrival when Jan's words brought her thoughts to an abrupt halt.

'I know you're not long returned from a trip, but you're the only woman we've got at the moment who knows Africa.'

'You want me to go to Africa?' Melanie echoed, then added, 'Who with?' as a suspicious and ungrammatical afterthought.

'It would be on your own. Do you think you could manage? It's a routine hand-holding job, a young woman in eastern Botswana as a volunteer who's had a bit of a breakdown—depression, not coping with the conditions, the climate, the people, and who knows what else? The volunteer organisation has asked us to bring her back.'

'Who is she with?' Melanie asked as her mind scooted ahead to the girl who had failed to adapt and enjoy what should have been a great adventure, the girl who was so miserable, so far from home.

'The same group you worked for,' Jan replied.

'That's why I thought you'd like to go. At least you'll be dealing with people over there that you've met before, and you'll know the set-up.'

'I'd love it,' Melanie told her, excited by the prospect of seeing her friends again. 'As long as you think I'll be able to handle it.'

'I'm certain you will. We'll organise the flights from here before you leave, and the organisation has undertaken to look after her until you arrive.'

'There's a flight each Thursday from Sydney to Harare, which is the closest international airport,' Melanie told her. 'Would it be possible to fly in and pick her up then fly out on the same day if they brought her that far?'

'I'll see what we can arrange with the organisation and talk to Bill about flights,' Jan said. 'You'd better see Peter for malaria prophylaxis in case you have to stay over, and speak to him about what sedatives you might need if she's overwrought.'

The moment has come, Melanie thought, steeling herself to face him with an efficient professionalism.

'He's in his office at the moment,' Jan added. 'You pop in and sort out the drugs while I get Bill busy on the flights and speak to the Volunteer Association about possible meeting places. If that flight still goes Thursdays you may have to leave here tonight and stay overnight in Sydney.'

Melanie forced herself to leave Jan's office with a semblance of enthusiasm. The prospect of going to Africa *must* outweigh the disadvantage of spending a few minutes with Peter!

He looked up at her, unsmiling, as she entered, and echoed Jan's question.

'Do you think you can manage?'

'I'm certain I can,' she responded, matching her mood to his with a businesslike crispness.

His eyelids dropped, shuttering his gaze, and he pushed a notepad uneasily about on his desk, bumping it against bottles of drugs before eventually focusing on the notes he had written on it.

'No doubt you're aware that falsiparum malaria is resistant to chloroquine in East Africa?'

Melanie nodded.

'As volunteers, we used chloroquine and Maloprim in combination—one tablet of Maloprim on Wednesdays and one of 300 mg of chloroquine on Sundays,' she explained.

'Starting the chloroquine a week before you left?'

Melanie nodded again, wondering what the difficulty was.

'You may not need anything, but in case you have to stay over you'll have to take precautions. All the usual treatments begin early, but you could take a low-dose doxycycline, which is often used for short-term stays in resistant areas. One 100mg capsule of Doryx each day with plenty of water,' he explained, lifting some capsules out of one of the bottles, dropping them into a glass vial and labelling it as he spoke.

'But if I'm going to turn around and come back on the same flight, it won't be necessary, surely? The plane arrives and departs in broad daylight, and I might not have to leave the air terminal. The danger lies in being outside between dusk and dawn.'

'You should still be prepared for anything,' he said sternly, and she bit back another futile argument.

She knew doxycycline was one of the tetracyclines, and they invariably gave her thrush, but that wasn't something she was about to discuss with Peter Wade.

Perhaps she could wait until she knew when they were coming back before taking the first tablet.

'Take one before you land, just in case,' he ordered, as if reading her rebellious mind. 'Who knows what will happen when you arrive? And, if your plans are disrupted, there's no guarantee you won't forget later. And if you stay, one every day, you understand?'

Yes, sir! she wanted to snap in response to his dictatorial tones, but she bit her tongue and contented herself with a nod as he moved on to antidepressant drugs she would be carrying for her patient.

'I'll give you Sinequan. It's a mild antidepressant effective on a wide range of psychoneurotic disorders including anxiety neurosis, which is probably this woman's problem.'

He was delving into a medical chest as he spoke, as if unwilling to look at her, or uninterested in anything more than the prescribing of a suitable drug.

'Wouldn't she have been receiving treatment already?' Melanie asked. 'It's not the end of the earth, and they do have hospitals and doctors in the larger towns.'

His head came up abruptly and he gazed across at her, as if perplexed by her statement.

'If she has been treated and has been on any of the monoamine oxidase inhibitors, then she'll have to continue to use them, as MAOI therapy must be discontinued at least a fortnight before using other drugs. I'll put a pharmaceutical reference book in the medical kit. You can check on any drug she's been prescribed and find any contra-indications or precautions. And don't hesitate to contact me if you're in any doubt.'

He paused, but she sensed that he hadn't finished.

'It's a one-person job, Melanie, but I must admit I'm not happy about you taking it.'

He doesn't trust me, she thought as despair lanced through her.

'I know many of the people who work for the organisation over there, and I've nursed in a psychiatric ward. I know a little of the language, and I should think I was the perfect choice.' She argued automatically, determined to hang on to this opportunity to prove her worth. 'As Jan said, it's a simple hand-holding job that needs a woman.'

It was his turn to nod, and as he looked up again his eyes scanned her face, as clear and unreadable as a summer sky.

'If she's deeply depressed, she could be suicidal, although the only report we've received to date hasn't indicated any attempts. Make sure you keep the drugs with you at all times. The case is small enough to fit into your hand luggage, and the vials could go into your handbag if you stay over and have to leave the hotel.'

She watched the frown twitch his eyebrows together and her mind slipped from the job ahead of her as she restrained an impulse to reach out and smooth the frown-lines away.

'You do understand,' he said sharply, and she reached out and picked up the tablets he had bottled instead.

'I won't let them out of my sight,' she assured him, and rose, knowing that to stay any longer would be courting more heartache.

'See Jan for flight arrangements and then go home and get organised. I'm still trying to contact the supervisor in Botswana and if I get any further details I'll let you know on the way to the airport.'

The last words halted her escape.

'I can drive myself to the airport and leave my car in the long-term car park.'

She forced out the words, although her heart was behaving most erratically as she wondered, with stupid hope, why he would choose to drive her.

'I'll take you out,' he said flatly. 'The girl is from Brisbane so you'll be bringing her back to here. One of the doctors will have to meet you anyway, to check out the patient before we hand her over to her family. Whoever meets you can drive you home.'

And that's that, she thought as her heartbeats decelerated in the light of this prosaic statement. She walked back to Jan's office, determined not to let her reactions to Peter affect the pleasure she felt in the prospect of going back to Africa.

'We've made two return bookings,' Jan told her as she came back into the room. 'One is for a same-day return, if we can organise the patient to be brought to the airport. The alternative is for a flight back via South Africa three days later. If that doesn't suit you, when the time comes, it would be worth waiting in Harare for the direct flight next week.'

'I hope I remember all this,' Melanie said, clutching her head theatrically as Jan poured out the information.

'You will, but it's all written down if you do need to confirm anything, and as you'll be phoning us every day, you can always call for extra help or ask Bill to reorganise your travel arrangements.'

Jan passed her a card with UniversAid's toll-free

number emblazoned on it, plus the time-differences between East Africa and Brisbane clearly marked.

'Now, about your patient,' she continued. 'Her name is Robyn Ryan, and she's a twenty-one-year-old student who has been away three months.'

'So the problem probably began soon after she arrived, and they've been coaxing her along thinking it was homesickness.'

'That's the most likely scenario,' Jan agreed, pushing a file across the desk. 'Here are copies of her application forms and the details of her interviews by the selection panel, her medical report from that time, and her references. It might give you some background that will be useful in getting her to talk—even if it's only about her family. Anything that takes her mind off the sense of failure she must feel will help.'

Melanie picked up the file and leafed through it.

'Now, if you've no more questions, I suggest you go home and pack what you'll need. You're booked on tomorrow morning's six-thirty flight to Sydney, and Peter has volunteered to be the one to see you off.' She smiled, as if relieved it wasn't to be her job!

'He'll call for you at five, and will have the tickets, credit cards, tentative hotel reservations and, hopefully, a proper medical report on Robyn from Botswana. OK?'

Jan's confidence in her radiated from her cheerful, smiling face, and Melanie smiled back. She had travelled alone often enough for it to hold no terrors, and she was certain she could handle her 'patient'. The only doubt was the farewell party, if you could call one person a party!

It's only a half-hour drive from my place to the airport, she told herself reassuringly as she drove back to her flat. I can manage that long in his company without falling to pieces.

Five o'clock in the morning was not a good time for resistance, Melanie decided as they drove through the deserted city towards the airport. Her body, still heavy with sleep, had reacted with a sensuous longing to snuggle up to him, to rub and press against him in the way cats did against the legs of those they favoured.

Her head, distracted by the effort of control, took refuge in a stolid silence. She was a courier, being dispatched on another mission, and she must act appropriately.

'Excited about going back to Africa?'

Had he asked the question to break the silence? she wondered. He certainly didn't appear to be interested in her answer, for he stared ahead, watching the traffic-free road with all the concentration of a Grand Prix driver on a dangerous circuit.

'As I'll probably be flying in and straight back out, there's not a lot to get excited about,' she told him, intending to match his disinterest with her own casual approach. Then the thought of going back to the warmth and colour, the vibrancy that seemed to light the air of Africa, triggered a tingling thrill.

'I suppose even someone in transit at the airport can walk outside and smell the place,' she added, smiling irrepressibly at the thought. 'Yes, I am excited!'

'You really enjoyed your time there?'

She had heard the amazement in people's voices before, but the utter astonishment in Peter's widened her smile.

'I loved it,' she said simply, 'the bits I saw of Central and East Africa. The people are friendly, and kind.

Gentle giants, someone once called them, and that's how I saw them.'

'Some of those same gentle giants are the children and grandchildren of the most feared warrior races on earth,' he objected, turning to look at her now with a teasing glint in his eyes.

'Every country on earth has had tribal wars and conflict between old and new settlers, going back as far as history records, and beyond.'

He was negotiating the roundabout that gave access to the airport drive, so did not reply, but the look he shot in her direction as they settled on to the wide, straight road had an indefinable, questioning quality as if something had surprised him. She thought over her words then shrugged the thought away.

He dropped her at the entrance then drove off to park the car while she queued for check-in and seat allocation. It was a relief to be away from him, she decided, but knew it wasn't true when she kept glancing around, eager to see him again before she left.

He caught up with her at the entrance to the departure lounge, and, taking her arm, led her to a quiet spot by the wide glass wall that provided a view out over the tarmac.

'I haven't been able to speak to the doctor who saw Robyn,' he said in a confidential undertone that sizzled into her ears like a secret message of some kind. 'I did speak to someone at the hospital where she was treated, but the story I got there was unsatisfactory.'

Melanie tried to look intelligent, although her hormones were stirring wildly, sparking flames that licked along her nerves as she felt his breath on her lips and savoured his maleness in her nostrils.

'I'll make sure someone from the organisation meets

you at the airport, whether the girl is with them or not. That way, you'll know immediately what's happening. If there's any change in status I'll get a message to you on the plane.'

Melanie was startled out of her preoccupation for an instant. Surely a simple operation like this did not need this level of military precision!

'The return tickets are in the travel wallet, there are everyday drugs like aspirin in the small medical bag, and the pharmaceutical guide is also in there.'

He was rattling off instructions like a robot, but there was nothing robotic about the messages his body was sending her. It had swayed closer as he spoke, so that only a thin layer of air separated them.

'You must ring as soon as you arrive and again before you leave. If you have to stay over, call every night. We need to know what's happening.'

She nodded, unable to speak. She knew all this, so why was he repeating it, drumming it in as if she were an imbecile?

Her head kept up a silent protest, as much to distract her attention from the agony of her body as for any other reason. The space between them was not the insulation she needed. A brick wall might have served the purpose, but three inches of air, zinging with electrical impulses, magnified her desire to lean against him, to ease her heavy, tingling breasts against his chest, and feel the hardness of his thighs against the aching centre of her femininity.

'And don't take any risks,' he was saying sternly when she dragged her mind back to his lecture. 'If the situation develops into anything you feel you can't handle, call for help. The volunteer organisation, the

local hospital, the police, call anyone. Don't try to
tough it out on your own, understand?'

She nodded again, upset that he sounded so angry
with her. It was as if he'd suddenly decided she was
incapable.

The thought acted on her aroused body as effectively
as a cold shower, and the fire she'd been battling
against sputtered and fizzed, dying beneath his vocal
irritation.

Yet his body still sent a different message, subtle but
strong. It cast a reel of silken thread around her,
holding her where she stood while it sang it's silent
need.

He's married! You're imagining things! If he liked
you, would he be speaking to you in this way? The
thought whirled around her head.

Half heard, his precise instructions continued, but
she was lost in the muddied waters of desire once more,
and battling against her own resurgent hunger.

'They've called my flight,' she blurted out, desperate
to escape yet unable to move.

'Yes, you've got to go,' he echoed hoarsely, yet
made no attempt to stand aside, or to release her from
the bondage of his sexuality. 'I don't want you to go,'
he said, when the silence straining between them had
reached snapping-point.

'I'm quite capable of flying to Africa and bringing
back a young woman who's depressed,' she said curtly,
and stepped backwards, unable to bear, for another
instant, the unspoken messages that battered her body.

Her heel caught against the window-frame, and she
tilted sideways as her leg gave way, but whether she
would have fallen remained a mystery, for his hands
reached out and seized her shoulders, pulling her across

the space that had been so ineffective a barrier, and holding her hard against him.

'Are you OK?' he asked after too long a moment, his voice soft and rasping, as if he had been running and was finding it hard to get enough breath to speak clearly.

'I'm fine. It was a silly stumble,' she said quickly, raising her hands from his shoulders and patting at her hair in an effort to distract his eyes from her flushed face. 'That's the final call; I've got to go.'

She stepped sideways this time, but his arms followed her, his hands still gripping tightly to her shoulders.

He's going to kiss me! she thought, her heartbeats accelerating wildly.

But the hands did not pull her forward, giving her instead a little shake.

'You've got to go,' he echoed, looking at her with the question in his eyes that she'd seen earlier, the question she couldn't understand. 'Remember to ring when you arrive,' he added, smiling determinedly at her puzzled face, his eyes clear and unreadable once again.

With his hands still touching her body, he turned her and pushed her gently towards the departure gate, and the smiling stewardesses who waited patiently for her to join the flight.

It probably looked like a lovers' farewell, she thought dismally, acknowledging their smiles with a wan effort of her own. A little last minute tête-à-tête, then a quick—or not so quick!—embrace.

Would they believe it if I told them it was strictly business? she wondered as she reached her seat and settled into it for the flight to Sydney.

Probably not!

Had her body believed it was strictly business?

Definitely not!

Her mind cantered around in circles as the plane taxied and thrust upwards into the blueness, asking and answering questions that had no relevance.

Hormones notwithstanding, her relationship with Peter *was* a business one—and that was how it had to remain.

CHAPTER EIGHT

AFRICA was as bright and beautiful as she remembered it, she decided as the plane circled above Harare. The dark green leaves of the tulip trees hid the bright orange flowers she knew were there and contrasted with the soft mauve of jacarandas in full bloom. Massive figs, poincianas and eucalypts reminded her of home, but the traffic jostling on the narrow strip of bitumen between the red dirt on the suburban roads told a different story as overladen buses veered around the constant flow of pedestrians. Bougainvillaea provided a riot of colour against the wide green lawns around the embassies and beautiful private gardens, and swimming-pools lay like blue jewels beneath the brightly burning sun.

Her heart lifted as the plane dropped from the sky.

This was what she loved about travel—the rising tide of half-fearful expectation of what might lie head, the continual challenge of journeying into unknown territory, of taking that first small step towards unimaginable pleasure and delights.

Could anything else compete with it? she wondered, as if to reassure herself that her ambitions were still in place.

Sex might, came a craven whisper from the part of her mind she'd shut down when she'd left Brisbane. Not just any sex, it hurried to assure her, but a satisfying sexual relationship with someone you really

loved, a giving and taking of pleasure that was in itself
as much a voyage into the unknown as this one was.

The wheels thudded into the ground, and her
thoughts came to an abrupt end.

For most of the journey, she'd managed to put Peter
and his bizarre behaviour firmly out of her mind,
repeating cautions to herself until she had forced her
brain and, hopefully, her body to accept them. And
now she was thinking not of love but of sex! All right,
she'd added love to the thought, but sex had come
first.

The plane slowed and stopped, and the scramble to
collect belongings began. She sat until the queue had
diminished to a few families waking tired children and
gathering up toys. Diplomats, most likely, she decided
as she shouldered her small bag and headed down the
aisle, wondering if she'd be back on the plane in a few
short hours.

'Melanie, it is very good to see you!' The rich,
velvety voice called to her above the heads of the
crowd as she came through the customs exit.

Ambrose had been her supervisor during her stay in
Botswana, and she flung her arms around his ample
figure and hugged him tightly, then looked around to
see if he'd had brought her 'patient'.

'I have spoken to your boss back in Australia,'
Ambrose told her quickly, reading the question in her
searching eyes. 'I have explained to him the circumstances and confirmed your booking at the hotel.'

He led the way towards the exit, and as the doors
slid open Melanie felt the blast of aromatic heat that to
her was the essence of Africa.

'So I'm not going back on today's plane?'

She breathed deeply, as if to rejuvenate all the cells of her body with the hot mysterious air.

'No!'

Ambrose bent to unlock the door of a battered old car, holding it open for her while she slid into the stifling interior.

'There's a problem?' she asked, as he settled in beside her.

'You might say that,' he answered cautiously, avoiding her eyes by concentrating on the road.

I'd forgotten that it takes patience to get the full story over here, she thought, while her mind scouted around for the most direct yet acceptable approach.

'Are you Robyn's supervisor?'

There was a short, sharp nod of confirmation.

'And is she here in Harare?'

Another nod.

'Is she well enough to travel?'

Again the dark head bobbed, though less decisively. It was time for a different kind of question.

'Where is she at the moment?' she asked, and watched his face to see if she could detect any changes in the placid mask.

'She's at the hotel.'

There was a pause long enough to be called an awkward silence, but Melanie had decided she'd asked enough. Finally, as the car turned into the wide main road and approached the large luxury hotel where she would be staying, he added the words he had not wanted to say.

'She doesn't want to go home, Melanie,' he told her, then clamped his lips closed again.

And you could hardly drag her kicking and screaming to the airport, Melanie realised, feeling a pang of sympathy for her old friend as she recognised the social and moral issues that had made his task impossible.

'I've got a booking home via South Africa, leaving here Sunday,' she told him. 'Perhaps by then I'll have persuaded her it's the sensible thing to do—even if I have to promise her she can come back again some other time.'

The fleeting look of horror on Ambrose's face was enough to make her wonder what Miss Robyn Ryan had been up to during her short time in Africa. If she was in a depressed state, suicide was the most likely medical emergency. Had she attempted it and per-suaded them to cover it up? The volunteer organis-ations had an obligation to report any illness affecting their workers at least to the headquarters in the volun-teers' home country. It was then up to the home base to decide if the information should be passed on to families.

'There is a nurse from an agency with Robyn,' Ambrose told her formally as he accompanied her up the steps and into the hotel. 'We have arranged for her to stay as long as you are here, to help you in caring for her.'

Melanie felt anxiety surge through her body. There was something more serious than a mild depression caused by homesickness wrong with Robyn if the organisation had arranged for a nurse to stay with her.

She glanced at Ambrose as she waited for the clerk to process her arrival, but the lugubrious expression on his face told her there was nothing more to be learnt from him.

'Will I see you again while I'm here?' she asked, hoping to win a smile. 'Perhaps you and Sylvie would like to come in and have dinner with me one night. To-morrow?'

In her own ears the question sounded like a plea, and she knew she was asking for his continuous support as she realised how alone she was going to be in the situation that lay ahead—except for the nurse from the agency, of course!

'I will ring you this evening,' was all the reply she was going to get. He put out his hand to shake a brief farewell. 'The nurse has my number if there is anything I can do,' he added, then turned and walked away, leaving her to follow the bellboy towards the lifts, and up to the suite booked by UniversAid before she'd left Australia.

Robyn Ryan was sitting in the small room that divided the two bedrooms. It was beautifully furnished with bright woven curtains that suggested native hand-crafts, ornately carved furniture, and a huge platter of gourds and fruit arranged as a centrepiece on a small dining table by the wall. Her prospective patient was watching an old American comedy show on television with an intensity it did not deserve.

In the other armchair, a nurse with the fine features of the Indians who had come to Africa as labourers generations earlier was watching her patient and the programme with equal concern.

'I'm Melanie Ashcroft,' she said brightly, stepping into the tableau with a quaking heart.

Her fellow professional rose to shake hands with her, but Robyn's attention remained riveted on the television screen. Assuming that the girl hadn't heard her, Melanie moved across to tap her on the shoulder and say, 'Hi,' in what she hoped was a confident and friendly tone.

Robyn remained immobile, ignoring the newcomer with a concentration that frightened Melanie.

'I'm Priti Kavansh,' the nurse said, covering the awkward silence with her own introduction. 'And this is Robyn.'

Still the girl ignored them and Melanie felt her discomfort growing although she hid it behind a bland unconcern.

'Which is my bedroom?' she asked, looking around the room so that the question was not directed at anyone in particular.

'It's through here,' Priti responded, opening the door that led off one side of the small room. 'There is a shower off it if you need to freshen up after your long flight.'

At least she's trying to ease the situation, Melanie thought, and rewarded her with a warm smile.

'I'll take you up on that. I feel like a grubby six-year-old after a particularly rough day at school.'

Priti smiled, but Robyn's attention hadn't wavered from the screen. Then, as Melanie moved to close the door behind her, she heard her say in a soft but determined voice, 'I am not going home!'

Well, that's nothing if not definite, she thought as she dragged off her travel-stained clothes and dug in her bag for clean ones. I suppose I should be grateful she's speaking to me at all!

As she stepped under the shower, she remembered Peter's instructions. 'Ring as soon as you arrive', he'd ordered. Well, she'd arrived, but apart from the fact that she wouldn't be returning on the same flight, which Ambrose had already told him, there was nothing else to report.

She'd ring this evening, when she had more idea of

what was going on in Robyn's mind, and maybe some slight clue as to how she could handle the situation.

Hot water streamed over her body, washing away the lethargy that long flights imposed. She shampooed her hair and was rinsing off the bubbles when the phone rang.

Would Priti answer it?

She turned off the water and listened, but the shrill summons continued. Pulling a thick towel around her body, she hurried through to the bedroom and picked up the extension by the bed.

'You were told to ring when you arrived,' Peter's furious voice spat into her ear.

'Ambrose had already advised you that I won't be on the return flight, and as our patient has refused to speak to me and I haven't had time to hear or see any medical reports it seemed pointless.'

She hoped she sounded calmer than she felt as irritation at his attitude and a devastating excitement at hearing his voice warred within her.

'You should have rung anyway, if only to let us know you arrived safely,' he said, his voice softer now, coming through the wires like a husky whisper that tingled across the nerve-endings in her skin. 'Do you have my home number?'

She shook her head, bemused by the question, then realised he couldn't see her response and replied with a doubtful, 'No'.

'Here it is.' He gave the list of numbers with a crisp edge to his voice, asking her to repeat what she had written, before adding a curt, 'Phone me later at home. I need to know what's happening over there.'

She heard the click that disconnected him and felt a

shadow of guilt. Had he been waiting at the office for her to call?

She checked her watch. It was only three hours since the plane had landed. Eleven in the evening at home. Perhaps he'd had other couriers checking in, which would explain why he was in the office so late.

Whatever the reason for his impatient call, it was a reminder that she was here to work. She dressed quickly and went through to join the other two women.

'Do you think we could have a talk about what you would like to do?' she asked Robyn, wondering if anything would distract her fixed attention from the television screen.

I've got three days before we have to leave; should I push this now? she wondered, thinking ruefully how excited she'd been by the 'challenge' of this job!

Priti stood up and indicated her chair, then slipped through the door that must lead to the second bedroom. Melanie sat down and focused on the show, recognising it as one she had seen as a child. She waited until an advertisement for a particularly impressive bicycle came on, and spoke again.

'Is there anything special you'd like to do this afternoon, Robyn? Have a wander round the shops, perhaps, or go to the native market?'

Did she imagine the movement or had the girl actually shuddered?

'It seems a boring way to spend a lovely day, cooped up inside watching television,' she added, and this time was rewarded with a response.

'I like it,' Robyn told her, her eyes never leaving the screen although the advertisement had changed to one extolling a particular brand of fertilizer for legume crops and was less than riveting.

So Melanie sat.

She'll have to go to the bathroom eventually, and I can talk to Priti then, she decided. Maybe if I have some background I'll be able to decide how to handle her.

The afternoon dragged on, and Priti returned, pulling up another chair, so the three of them sat in silence broken only by American-accented voices and canned laughter.

'Is there an especially good dining-room in the hotel, Robyn,' she asked as dusk darkened the room, 'or should we go out to eat? I've only driven past this place before. It was too expensive for me to visit when I was over here as a volunteer.'

She dangled the informtion in front of the girl, hoping it might stir her interest if the question about food was ignored, but the silence continued.

Melanie was pleased that Priti had declined to answer for Robyn, although words were obviously burning on her lips. She sat on, determined not to appear to give in to the stubborn silence, but her mind whirled as it sought for something that might open a chink in Robyn's armour of uninterest.

She was wondering how to organise a television malfunction, when her patient rose without a word and walked through to the bedroom.

'Has she been like this since you met her?' she whispered to Priti.

'Just the same,' the other nurse sighed. 'The doctor at Mahalapye gave her tablets, and at first, Ambrose said, she talked about things she had done and seen during her stay. Then they got back here to Harare, in the traffic and noise, and she became very upset,

saying, "Take me to a hotel, take me to a hotel," all
the time.'

'Ambrose would have loved that!' Melanie said with
a grin that won a similar response from Priti. 'So he
brought her here?'

'Yes, and phoned the agency to arrange a nurse to
stay with her. It was only yesterday, but I can't get her
to talk or to go outside. She sits here and watches the
television all the time, even through the night, as if
she's afraid to sleep. We've had meals sent up, and
she's eating well. It will be costing your company a
great deal in a place like this!'

Concern darkened her beautiful eyes, and Melanie
hastened to reassure her.

'The company won't complain about that—as long
as I get her safely home. If she refuses to travel, I'm
not certain what I can do.'

She wondered about getting help from the embassy,
and cursed her own inexperience. She was supposed to
be able to think on her feet, to come up with alternatives until she found something that would work. If she
wanted to prove she was the best apprentice
UniversAid had ever had, she would have to find a way
through the problem.

'I think we'll start by turning off the television,' she
announced as she heard the toilet flush and realised
that Robyn would be back with them shortly.

Robyn came back into the room, her eyes going
automatically to the blank screen. She walked across
to turn it back on, but Melanie stepped in front of her.

'I thought we might leave it off for a while,' she said
quietly. 'It will give us all a chance to talk, to get to
know each other. Television is the most unsociable of
all mankind's inventions.'

'I don't have to talk to you,' Robyn muttered, pushing Melanie aside to reach the television switch.

'I think you do.' Melanie swung back into her path, and looked her straight in the eye. 'UniversAid is paying the bill here, Robyn, and as I represent them I think I should have some rights. I'm not turning it off for good,' she added calmly as a flush of anger rose in the other woman's pale cheeks, 'just for ten minutes while we talk about possible plans.'

There was a split-second between her realisation that there was more wrong with Robyn than mild depression and the forceful shove that sent her reeling back into the television set, knocking it off its stand with a shattering explosion of glass and the sparking sound of electricity suddenly let loose.

Priti flicked the switch at the wall then rushed towards her as she lay awkwardly across the broken set, but Melanie waved her urgently away, towards the door through which Robyn had disappeared.

'See where Robyn's gone. If she leaves the hotel, ask one of the staff to go with you and follow her if you can. With two of you, one can stop and ring here to let me know what's happening.'

Priti ignored her frantic waving and reached out to steady her as she stood up. 'She'll be in the bedroom,' the nurse asssured her. 'I'll check for you, but that's where she'll be. She won't go out! Whatever it is that's worrying her is tied up with the outside world. It's as if she's found this little hole and crawled into it for safety.'

Melanie listened carefully, thinking through what Priti was saying. It made sense, particularly as Robyn's agitation had increased when Ambrose had driven into the city.

She had known enough about her condition to ask
him to get her to a hotel. Was it agoraphobia?

'And the television is shutting out the things she
doesn't want to think about, even here, in the safety of
the hotel?' she said slowly.

Priti nodded. 'I think so.'

'Then we'd better get another one, I suppose,'
Melanie said, looking down at the shattered mess with
a rueful grin.

It was then that she felt a hot, wet stickiness running
down her arm and on to her fingers. She twisted around
to see the gash down the back of her triceps. Long, but
not deep, she decided, and hurried into the bedroom
for a towel to staunch the flow before she spread blood
all over the hotel suite.

'I'll check on Robyn then come back and bind it for
you,' Priti told her, pushing her into a sitting position
on the bed.

And what am I supposed to do? Ring Peter and
admit I can't handle the situation? Melanie lifted the
receiver, then put it down. Pride made her determined
to find a solution. She had time on her side. Somehow
she had to get through to Robyn, to convince her that
she was a friend, here to help her out of the dark maze
her mind had fashioned for her.

She looked up as Priti came back into the room with
wadding and plaster. She must have her own emergency kit, Melanie thought, then turned to her as a
fellow professional.

'Have you any ideas about how I should handle this?'

'I haven't much experience with psychiatric problems, but perhaps a specialist?'

'Do you know one you could recommend?'

'I know a man who is considered highly at the hospital where I worked, but. . .'

Priti's voice trailed away.

'But what, Priti?' Melanie asked, unable to understand this sudden reversion to silence.

'He is a native and I don't know how much of Robyn's problem is to do with black people, and how much with people in general.'

The words, blurted out with embarrassment, made Melanie think, but there were obvious discrepancies in this concern.

'But she doesn't get agitated by your presence, and Ambrose drove her back to the city——'

'Maybe she knew Ambrose before whatever happened that triggered this.'

Melanie shook her head, tiredness creeping through her bones as she realised the futility of their guessing game.

'We could keep this up for days,' she admitted. 'What we need is an expert.'

Should she ring the office back in Brisbane and ask if they had anyone to suggest? You're on your own, Melanie, she reminded herself. If the office wasn't there at the end of the telephone line, what would you do?

'I'll ring the embassy first,' she told Priti, answering her own question, 'and see if they can recommend a psychiatrist. Maybe they know of a white woman who practises here,' she added with a grin. 'Or, better still, a woman like yourself. I obviously aggravate Robyn far more than you do.'

She reached for the phone and was soon talking to an English-speaking psychiatrist from Brussels, wife of a businessman in the city, who ran a small clinic on the outskirts of Harare, and also served most of the ex-patriot population when their isolation drove them towards neuroses.

'I'll come over in an hour,' she assured a grateful Melanie, agreeing to stay and have dinner with them in the hope that Robyn might be more forthcoming in a social atmosphere.

'You said Robyn had been treated by a doctor in Mahalapye. Did Ambrose give you a medical report from him?' she asked after she had explained the position to Priti.

'Robyn had it, but threw it away at some stage, as far as we can make out. She is on——' Priti fished in her pocket and produced a small bottle of tablets '—Nortab, 25mg three times a day. It's nortriptyline,' she added, reading from the label. 'Do you know it?'

'No, but I'll look it up in a moment. Does she object to taking them?'

Priti shook her head. 'I give her one with meals, and so far she hasn't objected. Ambrose said they were to ease the depression, but they seem to agitate her.'

'So it could be the tablets causing the problems.'

It was a medical problem beyond her capabilities, she decided, and was thankful she'd called for help.

Elise Charpentier was a petite blonde with sparkling blue eyes. She brought with her an aura of calm confidence that worked on Melanie's tattered nerves like a soothing balm.

Another television had been delivered to the sitting-room, and Robyn was persuaded to join them, greeting Elise with a sullen nod.

'Shall we order dinner to be brought up, or would

you like to go down to the dining-room?' Melanie
asked her, hoping to get some response.

'Perhaps we should eat here,' Elise suggested, her
eyes on her new patient, taking in the untidy hair and
the dull eyes. 'Is there a room-service menu?'

It was the first positive response Melanie had seen
Robyn make, for she grabbed the patterned card that
held the menu, and studied it with a greedy intensity.
As the phone rang again, Melanie left them to it, and
walked through to her bedroom to answer it.

Peter's temper hadn't improved.

Quietly Melanie explained what was happening,
pointing out to him her intention to ring him as soon
as Elise had spent time with Robyn and suggested
possible courses of action.

'Has she been on medication?' he barked into the
phone, and Melanie told him what had been
prescribed.

'I haven't had time to check on it in the book yet,'
she said feebly, feeling that somehow she was failing in
this major test.

'I can tell you it's a drug that's commonly used for
mild depressive states. The difficulty with it and other
MAOIs is that if the patient is misdiagnosed, which
can easily happen, and the depression is a phase of
something more complicated, it can trigger latent
schizophrenia or manic depression.'

'Oh, great!' Melanie said bitterly. 'That's more
believable than the original diagnosis.' She rubbed at
her bandaged arm. 'So what do we do?'

'Leave it to the psychiatrist. You did the right thing
getting on to her immediately. Give her my number
and get her to ring me when she's come to some
conclusion, or, better still, ask her to ring me from the

hotel before she leaves. That way I can talk to you both.'

Melanie checked her watch.

'It's two a.m. at home, Peter,' she objected. 'There's nothing you can do that can't wait till morning. Why don't you get some sleep?'

'You've been up as long as I have,' he reminded her. 'Just ring me, Melanie!'

It was an unmistakable order!

'I will,' she promised, then was devastated when he mumbled,

'I shouldn't have let you go!' into the phone before he hung up.

He doesn't think I can cope. The thought hammered in her head, making her more determined than ever to bring Robyn home safely.

Three hours later she was wondering if commitment was worth the pain.

Priti had handed Robyn her tablet at the beginning of the meal, generating a tension in Melanie that she found hard to dispel. Was Elise watching her patient as warily? She had certainly looked at the tablets and nodded her understanding of the prescription. Had the idea of the drug triggering some latent problem occurred to her? She wished she'd had an opportunity to speak to Elise alone, but had not wanted to interrupt the doctor's tentative forays into friendship with Robyn.

The four of them had enjoyed a delicious dinner, with all but Robyn entering into the pretense that it was a normal social occasion. Elise entertained them with stories about her travels through Central Africa, and Melanie contributed snippets of her adventures in Botswana. Priti had asked questions about Australia, and they had relaxed back into their chairs, sipping at their coffee, when the explosion occurred.

Robyn had pushed aside her coffee-cup with an abrupt movement that rattled the china and risen to her feet. She looked around, and her eyes seemed to register the replacement television set. She strode towards it.

Priti shrugged her shoulders as if to say, Well, we managed to keep it off for a while, and Elise put her hand on Melanie's arm as she murmured, 'Let's see what she does.'

It was hardly what they had expected, for the woman seized the largest gourd from the platter that had been placed on the television set while they used the table for dinner, and swung it viciously downwards smashing through the screen with a demonic force that terrified the onlookers.

Then she whirled around, once, twice, three times, like a discus-thrower gathering momentum and the shapely object flew through the air towards the table.

'Ring hotel security,' Melanie managed to gasp as she leapt to her feet to shield Elise. She pushed Priti, who had also risen, towards the door, then the missile hit her head and the world went black.

She came to under the table, her head resting on Elise's knee, while the decorative arrangement was reduced to a litter of broken pieces around their feet.

'Stay still, we're fairly safe here,' Elise whispered. 'She's getting her fun throwing things. I don't think she's at all homicidal.'

'That's a comfort,' Melanie retorted, feeling the tender lump on the side of her forehead. 'I'm glad those things dry out to such light shells.'

'I've a sedative injection with me that I'll give her if

Priti manages to get enough help to hold her, then we'll have to admit her to hospital and see if we can stabilise her. You certainly won't get an airline to take you home while she's in this state.'

A book fluttered towards them, followed by the large menu. She was running out of things to throw! What would she decide to do next?

'Do you think the drugs were a trigger?' Melanie stilled her fear with the whispered question as a cushion joined the flying objects.

'I'd say almost certainly,' Elise whispered back, then sighed. 'It's a problem because residual effects of the drugs she's been on will react against many of the controlled drugs we could give her now. It will have to be done carefully and in a controlled situation. You understand that?'

Melanie nodded, and at that moment the door from her bedroom began to open, and Elise clutched at her arm and pointed at the main entrance and the other bedroom door. They were also opening cautiously.

'Can I talk to you for a moment, Robyn?' Priti asked, wisely using the door as a shield as another cushion flew through the air towards her.

She must have signalled to the security people, for two women and a man slipped into the room and moved purposefully towards the distraught traveller.

The scream she gave as they took hold of her arms curdled Melanie's blood and made all the hairs on the back of her neck prickle to attention. Forgetting her aching head, she crawled out from under the table and helped Elise to her feet.

'Priti, would you call an ambulance, please?' Elise asked quietly, ignoring the screams that ricocheted around the room like an unearthly siren. She walked across to collect the small briefcase she'd brought with her, and with steady fingers and an apparent lack of concern filled a small syringe and moved towards the girl who twisted desperately in the grip of her captors.

'This will make you feel better, Robyn,' she said calmly, her slightly accented English mellowing the words. 'We'll take you to hospital and look after you there.'

Melanie looked away, unable to bear the sight of Robyn's face, contorted in a rictus of fear. There was nothing else that they could do, she knew that, but a sense of failure descended on her like a black cloud.

The drug worked quickly. One minute the helpers held a fighting machine of superhuman strength, and the next a limp, almost comatose patient, who was helped tenderly to a chair and eased into it as the pity all of them felt went out to her in gentle kindness.

'Can I go to the hospital with her?' Melanie asked.

'Only if you want that head of yours X-rayed,' Elise replied, reaching out to feel the tender spot above Melanie's temple. 'I don't think it's necessary, but I would prescribe a good night's sleep and an easy day tomorrow.'

'But Robyn is my responsibility,' she objected, and was rewarded with a smile.

'Not now, she isn't,' Elise told her. 'She's my patient. I will go to the hospital and admit her, then speak with colleagues about her case. As with any patient in such a fragile state, I will not allow visitors for a few days.'

'But——'

'No buts, Melanie,' Elise told her as the ambulance attendants arrived with an extremely worried hotel manager. 'You go to bed, and I will ring you in the morning. Give me your boss's phone number and I will also ring him and tell him what is happening. I think Priti should stay with you for the night, in case you suffer a delayed reaction to the bump on your head. OK?'

Melanie smiled and nodded. Suddenly she was pleased to be told what to do. Her own brain had stopped working, but whether from tiredness or over-load she couldn't decide!

CHAPTER NINE

THEY came home on the direct flight to Sydney a week later, Robyn so heavily drugged that she slept every time she sat down. Melanie woke her for meals, and her heart went out to the docile woman who was now pathetically grateful for Melanie's assistance.

Unable to remember her stay at the hotel, she had accepted Melanie as a friend sent to bring her home, and she'd turned to her with a dependency that filled Melanie with a deep sadness.

As the plane circled above the blue-grey waters of Botany Bay, waiting for landing instructions, one of the stewards slipped into the vacant seat beside the two women.

'There's a message for you to stay on the plane. Someone from the Airport Medical Service will be coming on board and will help you through Customs and transfer you to your domestic flight.'

Melanie felt a surge of relief. She had been worrying about her ability to prop Robyn up for the time it would take to get through immigration procedure.

'Thanks,' she murmured to the man, who nodded understandingly and left as the plane touched down.

She watched the other passengers troop off, glad that she would be leaving on her own. In spite of the week in Harare, the black eye she'd developed as a result of the flying missile attack was now an interesting rainbow of yellow, dull green and purple. Not the sort

of face to be showing in public! she decided, then she
stood up and spun around at the sound of her name.

Or was it at the sound of his voice?

Peter was belting up the aisle towards her, his long
strides betraying anxiety, his face pale and drawn.

'I didn't expect you to be the medical help that was
coming on board,' she cried as tears of relief poured
down her cheeks.

'Melly!' he groaned, and his arms came round her,
holding her close against his chest and he ran his hands
over her body as if to assure himself that she was all
there. 'Oh, Melly!' he muttered again, his lips pressed
against her hair and his arms tightening into bands of
steel that cut into her flesh and squeezed the air from
her lungs.

Dazed, yet delighted by this unorthodox reception,
she snuggled against him, drawing a strength from his
warmth while her head whirled with a million questions
and her body began to flicker with desire.

A stewardess trying to get past brought them both
back to the present, and Peter turned her, still in his
arms, to allow the intruder to pass. Then one hand left
her back and reached up to lift her chin, and he cursed
under his breath when he saw her face, then brushed
the tears from her cheeks with long fingers that
trembled against her skin.

'I should never have let you go,' he said, his lips a
thin white line in his grim face. 'Never, you hear?' he
added, shaking her as if to emphasise the point as his
fingers brushed against her bandaged arm.

'Customs are waiting for you,' the stewardess called
from the back of the plane, and Melanie sat back down
in her seat and shook Robyn awake.

'We're nearly home,' she said, and all the joy of

Peter's presence was lost as she realised the words had no meaning for the girl. She looked up at Peter with all the aching doubt vivid in her eyes.

'She'll understand when the effect of the drugs wears off,' Peter said briskly, reading her thoughts as clearly as if they were written on a blackboard.

'But what if she's always on a dosage that dulls her to this extent?' she asked as the tears started to seep down her cheeks again, but whether because of concern for Robyn or disappointment that his manner towards her had changed she did not know.

'Get your bags, Melanie, and go on through Customs,' was Peter's abrupt response, the words cool enough to jolt Melanie out of the moment of pity. 'Will you recognise her luggage?'

'It's a brown backpack,' Melanie responded automatically to the businesslike tone that was such a contrast to his earlier warmth. Was he regretting the emotion-charged reunion? Was he angered by his momentary loss of control?

'Good! You get hold of it and put it through with your own carry-on bag, and I'll bring Robyn.'

The words jolted into her head. This is work, that's what he's saying, Melanie thought sadly as she walked through to the emptying customs hall. But why had he rushed to her and held her so tightly?

It wasn't as if she'd been in any danger. Once Robyn had been admitted to hospital, she'd had a pleasant week in Harare, but the excitement she'd expected to feel had been tempered by a longing to get home. It had been more like a holiday than work, although she had spent a lot of time with her patient after Elise had stabilised her.

And it wasn't as if he hadn't known she was safe!

She had rung the office every morning, as instructed, speaking to Jan or one of the telephone operators. Added to which, he had phoned her himself most evenings, to hear about her latest visit to the hospital and check on her patient's progress.

She collected the brown backpack and carted it over to a waiting customs officer, explaining the situation as she dropped her own small bag beside it.

She'd begun to look forward to Peter's phone calls, had collected snippets of information to pass on to him—to keep him talking longer. It was simply that he was a link with home, she'd repeatedly assured herself, ignoring the skipping beat of her heart whenever the phone had rung.

And Peter?

She turned to watch him come into the hall, supporting Robyn with a strong arm around her waist. Robyn was chatting to him, as alert as Melanie had seen her, but instead of feeling pleased she was aggravated by their closeness.

He's not for you, she told herself as the customs inspector rifled through the gear in Robyn's bag.

But the phone calls hadn't been entirely necessary, her heart argued, setting up a rhythmic tattoo as the pair drew nearer. And something in the way he had lingered, prolonging the conversation, had suggested more than the caring concern of an employer.

'All set?' the source of all her problems asked cheerfully as a small motorised buggy with a medical sign emblazoned on its side drews up beside them.

'You're clear here,' the customs officer announced, and Peter seated Robyn gently in the buggy while the driver dropped the two bags in the back and waved an arm for Melanie to climb into the back seat beside her patient.

'I'm taking you across to the domestic terminal,' he announced as he manoeuvred the silent vehicle out of the hall and on to the tarmac, where maintenance vehicles ran around under the wings of the huge jets like chickens at the feet of squat hens.

'Beats the bus,' Melanie told him, peering around with interest to keep her mind off the conundrum that was Peter.

'You take Robyn up to departure lounge fifteen,' he told her as they disembarked from their unorthodox transport. 'I'll check her bag in and get our seat allocation, then come on up and join you.'

There was a tentative smile on his lips, but his eyes held a gravity that frightened her. In fact, he looked—uncertain? She looked again. Well, maybe 'confused' was a better word. For a fleeting moment she thought he looked almost as confused as she felt, but what he had to be confused about she couldn't fathom.

Unless he, too, felt the electricity that permeated the air between them, the impulses as charged as lightning bolts that sent *frissons* of fear along her nerve-paths!

She grasped Robyn's arm and led her away, chatting cheerfully as she guided the girl through the crowds. This was no time to be worrying about things she could not understand—least of all *frissons* of anything. The word must have bobbed into her head from the book she'd been reading on the plane trip home!

She concentrated on her charge. It was the first time Robyn had been faced with a large crowd of people since she'd left hospital, as special arrangements had been made to seat them early on the plane from

Harare. Would she react in spite of the drugs that were depressing the action of her central nervous system?

Melanie could feel a building tension in the tightening muscles of the arm she held. She spoke reassuringly, but was immensely relieved when a member of the ground crew came forward to meet them as they reached the departure lounge.

'You can go straight on board,' the smiling woman said. 'They've rung through from the front desk to ask me to look out for you and see you seated up the front.'

'Spoilt, that's what we are, Robyn,' she said gaily, hurrying her past the waiting crowd in the wake of the stewardess.

She felt the relaxation in the girl as soon as they were safely on board, and made a mental note to tell Peter that they should wait until everyone was off before leaving the plane in Brisbane.

'Everything OK?' he asked, sliding into the seat beside her a little later, with the same anomalous smile she'd seen earlier hovering on his lips.

Maybe it was more anticipatory than puzzled!

Her body was not confused by smiles. Its welcome leapt in her blood, so tantalisingly alive, she was certain he must be able to feel the bubbling intoxication.

'Thanks to you,' she murmured as calmly as her catching breath would allow. 'I thought for a moment the crowd waiting to board might upset her, but the stewardess whisked us straight through.'

If he wanted businesslike, then that was what he'd get, although the effort to appear composed was overwhelming!

'And we'll disembark last in Brisbane,' he said, anticipating her warning.

Think about your patient, the remaining scrap of sanity in Melanie's head prompted. Robyn had closed her eyes again, and Melanie slid a finger around her wrist and felt her pulse, pleased to feel the steady rhythm.

The activity in the cabin had ceased as passengers strapped themselves into seats, and the plane began to roll forward. They sat in silence while the stewardess repeated the safety instructions, and the massive engines roared as they lifted the plane off the ground. Robyn, unfazed by what was happening, slid sideways in her seat, and drifted off to sleep once again.

'You did an excellent job in every way,' Peter told her when the noise died down and the aircraft levelled out at its flying height. The special warmth she thought she had heard over the phone deepened his voice, and his closeness radiated heat into her skin.

'I came close to panicking,' she admitted, embarrassed by his praise, 'and would have been lost if I hadn't found Elise.'

'But you reached out for help and you found it. No one could have handled it better.'

The words sent a shiver of delight through her body and she turned to him impulsively, her hand reaching out to grip his arm.

'Does this mean I've passed all the tests? Does it mean you'll take me on permanently?'

The muscle tensed beneath her hand, and he looked into her face. The warmth and softness she fancied she had seen in his eyes and heard in his voice disappeared.

'Does the job mean so much to you, Melly?' he asked gravely, and the shock of the question stopped her breath in her throat.

He was going to fail her!

'Of course it does!' she told him as despair mustered a courage she'd forgotten she had. 'It combines the two things I love more than anything—travel and work. It gives me a sense of achievement, being able to help people, even over the phone, when they are feeling desperate. It's a wonderful job and I've worked hard at it, and I can't think of one decent reason for you to turn me down!'

She glared her defiance at him, but his only reply was a tense frown and a quiet, 'Can't you, Melly?' uttered with such gravity that she could find no answer.

She battled against the tears that were burning behind her eyes, and turned to look past Robyn and out of the window, until the stewardess leaned towards them offering tea or coffee.

'I'll have a coffee, please,' she said, the words tumbling out as she bit back an angry denunciation of his behaviour, his perfidy—his calling her 'Melly'!

'Your two-month trial has a few days to go yet. Before deciding, I'd like——' He stopped suddenly, as if fearing he would say too much, then the stewardess was passing down their coffee and the moment was lost.

Melanie felt her stomach clench into a tight ball, but she forced herself to reach out for her cup with steady hands. The way she felt in Peter's presence was hardly conducive to good employer-employee relations anyway, she told herself, sipping at the bitter brew. She would probably have turned the job down even if he had deigned to make it permanent.

But disappointment as bitter as the coffee churned inside her, and a sense of injustice flared alongside it, fuelling her sense of outrage.

She thought of the channels open to her to fight for

her right to be employed, and was engaged in an imaginary conversation with the equal opportunities commissioner, when his hand brushed against her arm, and her blood began to sizzle in her veins.

She couldn't fight Peter!

'I was saying,' he began tentatively, looking anywhere but at her although his body was still bombarding hers with unspoken messages, 'that I'd like an opportunity to speak privately with you before that decision is made, Melanie.'

His voice was so correctly, formally *English* that it chilled her, even while the beautiful cadence of it sent shivers of delight tingling to the very tips of her toes.

What do you mean? she wanted to ask, but something told her she might not like the answer.

He was still studying the interior of the plane as if inspecting it for flaws, so she ignored the statement, and lost herself in chaotic thoughts.

Something also told her that she hadn't imagined the warmth in his voice over the phone each night, nor mistaken the ardour of his greeting. Could it be that Peter was every bit as attracted to her as she was to him? For, in spite of her lack of experience in such matters, she was certain that the sensory darts and pinpricks that stirred her blood to flame whenever he touched her must be reacting on him to some degree. Such electricity couldn't all be a one-way current, surely!

But what could he offer?

She almost laughed aloud. Laughed, because what she really wanted to do was cry.

Was he going to ask her to be his mistress? Was that it?

If that was what he wanted to discuss, she could

understand his reluctance to have her on the staff, she realised bitterly. It would be far too awkward for him, conducting an affair in full view of his employees!

Disappointment quenched the stupid licks of flame and dimmed her hope. It was as if her knight in shining armour had turned to face her, and she'd found him— rusty! Tarnished by his own weakness and duplicity.

'I'll drive you home when we've handed Robyn over to her family,' he said at last, his voice a hoarse croak, as if her thoughts had cut him back down to something small and uncertain. 'Maybe we can talk then if you're not too tired. I don't seem able to explain—to talk to you properly—in public like this!'

Melanie banished the instant rush of pity his words, and the pathetic tone in which they were issued, provoked. Men played on women's sympathies to get what they wanted. It was the oldest ploy in the book.

Ignoring his offer, she turned her face away from him and her mind back to her rehearsal of her conversation with the equal opportunities commissioner, strengthening her case with a defiant bravado that hid an aching heart.

Then Brisbane spread beneath them, and she began to wonder if she could slip away while he was speaking to Robyn's family, and take a taxi home.

'Robyn's booked into a private clinic here in Brisbane,' her nemesis said calmly, reverting to his business persona with an ease that exasperated her. 'They are sending a car and a trained nurse to the airport to take Robyn and her family back to the clinic together.'

'It's a shame she can't go straight home, but I can understand their taking precautions.' She remembered the violence of the woman's attack and shuddered, although her hand, as she shook Robyn awake, was gentle and her heart prayed for her charge's recovery.

The crowd of people greeting passengers had thinned by the time they disembarked. A woman in her fifties rushed towards them and folded Robyn in her arms, leading her towards a bank of chairs, while the man with her walked awkwardly beside the pair, his arms held out as if to shield them both.

Beyond them, as she followed, Melanie saw Kip's beaming smile, and realised with a sinking heart that Barry was with her.

'So the boyfriend that isn't has materialised again.'

The harsh words slapped against her, jolting her to a standstill so that his body cannoned into hers.

'Well, at least it saves me driving you home and making a fool of myself,' he muttered into her ear, then turned away and strode over to speak to the nurse who stood watching the family reunion with a broad smile.

'Do you have any baggage? Do you have to sign off or anything, or can we take you straight home?'

Kip's words flew like bullets from her lips, and Melanie wondered, as she kissed them both warmly, what had happened to cause such excitement. It wasn't just her return home, that was certain!

'You've been coming and going, and we've barely seen you, but something so unbelievable has happened, Mel,' Kip blurted out as they packed into her small car, Melanie taking the back seat as Barry walked around to the driver's side.

Melanie looked at her friend in surprise. Kip's enthusiasm for causes and concerns was well known to her, but this was something special. She glowed and bubbled, and even looked as if she'd lost some weight. There was a curious difference about her.

'You'd better tell me,' she said drily, thinking that she could use some good news given the ominous statements her boss had been throwing at her lately.

'Can't you guess?' Kip demanded, twisting around to face her as Barry pulled up to pay the parking charge.

'I've been travelling all day, Kip,' Melanie excused herself. 'It's hardly conducive to rational thought, nor a good preparation for Twenty Questions.'

'It's Barry and me!' Kip announced triumphantly, and Melanie saw the flush rising in Barry's neck. 'We're in love, aren't we?'

She tugged his arm and he nodded a silent corroboration of her news, while he concentrated on easing the car into the flow of traffic. Once this was negotiated he flicked a rather shamefaced smile over his shoulder at Melanie, as if confirming what Kip had said and apologising to her at the same time.

'But that's lovely!' Melanie exclaimed, realising that an appropriate reaction was expected of her. 'I'm really pleased for you both,' she added, although her heart was filled with sadness and her body felt heavy with pain.

She did not envy Kip her happiness, and Barry was a worthy suitor for her. It was partly because Barry was a pleasant chap that she herself had been unable to get rid of him, not wanting to hurt his feelings with a harsh finality.

'It started the night he came over—before you went to the States,' Kip was explaining, and Melanie sat half-listening while part of her mind pointed out that it meant she would be on her own now, another friend paired off! 'We talked and talked, and something sparked between us.'

'That's great!' Melanie said feebly, knowing the enthusiasm she expressed in the two words was too lukewarm to be acceptable. Or was Kip too much in love to notice?

'With you being away so much, I was wondering if you'd mind if Barry moved into the flat.'

Kip's words underlined Melanie's images of loneliness.

'We'd keep your room for you and you can still use it as a base, but once you're appointed to permanent staff you'll be travelling more and more.'

Which is what I thought I wanted, Melanie told herself, wondering why the idea lacked all appeal at the moment.

Was it because she no longer believed the permanent job would be hers, or because she was tired, or because. . .?

Kip's voice rattled on, but Melanie was lost in her own tangled thoughts. Could it be that she was jealous of Kip's happiness? Was it possible that love and marriage might suddenly be a more appealing dream for the future than work and travel?

Her heart turned over and she bent forward in her seat, shivering slightly as the dreadful doubts assailed her. She wrapped her arms around her suddenly cold body, and watched the river through the delicate tracery of jacaranda boughs and flowers, the colours taking her back to Africa, where life had seemed much less complicated and Peter's voice over the phone each night had planted a tiny seed of hope in her heart.

It had withered now, that seed. He hadn't even said goodbye to her when she'd left the airport, engrossing himself in a conversation with the nurse, as if he were the one who had brought Robyn home.

She had slept for most of her three days off, but felt little benefit from it as she rode up in the lift with one of the telephone staff on her return to work. As she watched Julie slide the metal plate into the slot that would allow the lift to stop on their floor, she realised she had lost the excitement of her ambitions.

Two months ago, her sights had been set on the day she would receive her own plate and be able to send the lift skyward. It had become the symbol of success to her, but now she wondered if she would ever be given one—or if she would ever use it, if she was.

Jan called to her as she walked towards the control-room, and she turned back, pleased that she didn't have to walk past Peter's office just yet.

'Would you like to use Peter's office to do your written report on the trip?' Jan asked. 'He's away at the moment, and you'll find it quieter than the control room. Here's a report from the doctor who is treating Robyn at the moment. I think you'll find it interesting.

Melanie picked up the sheaf of papers Jan pushed across the desk, praying that the prognosis would be better than she'd allowed herself to hope.

'You'll see he hasn't diagnosed schizophrenia, although onset during adolescence and early adulthood is common and being in an isolated situation could trigger a latent disorder. He's hoping it was an isolated incident of an affective disorder and is doing a full range of tests to try to rule out the common medical illnesses that can present as psychiatric disorders. There are metabolic and endocrine disorders, cardio-vascular causes like lupus and also severe systemic infections that could cause mental instability.' Jan added quietly, 'So don't despair yet! Add this preliminary paper to your report, and we should have another file from the doctor before the debriefing.'

'It's a dreadful thing to say, I suppose, but I do hope they find a nice treatable disease.'

'So do I,' Jan told her. 'Schizophrenia is not something you'd wish on your worst enemy.'

Her gaze swept over the fading bruises on Melanie's face, and concern darkened her eyes.

'Are you certain you feel fit enough to come back to work?' she probed. 'You still look very tired. Drained, almost!'

'Thanks!' Melanie said. 'That's all I need!'

The edge of bitterness in the words shocked even herself. Jan didn't deserve that.

'I'm sorry,' she added, with a wry shake of her head. 'Nothing seems to be going right at the moment, but that's no reason for me to take out my bad temper on you.'

'That's OK,' Jan assured her. 'But I hope you're not feeling out of sorts over some imagined failure in Zimbabwe. I don't know one of our couriers who would have handled that situation any better. I'm extremely proud of my protégée, although I died a thousand deaths when I realised the volatile situation I'd plunged you into.'

'You weren't to know that Robyn's condition was likely to deteriorate so badly.'

'No,' Jan agreed, 'but, believe me, there was no way I could convince Peter of that. If there'd been less complicated travel arrangements, I think he'd have been over there the next day, especially after we heard you'd been injured.'

Jan spoke in such a prosaic way, she made his concern sound normal, but her eyes, still scanning Melanie's face, seemed to be looking for clues.

'I wasn't badly injured,' Melanie protested. 'More colour than pain!' She rubbed the side of her face ruefully, while she battled against an impulse to ask Jan where Peter had gone. 'I'd better get on with the report,' she said, moving back from Jan's desk.

'Then take some more time off if you'd like it,' Jan told her, but Melanie shook her head. To be in the small flat while Barry and Kip billed and cooed at each other was more than she could bear.

Peter's office was too full of him! She ran her hand over the soft leather of his chair, imagining the imprint of his body on the hide, and the hairs on her arms stood on end with an electrifying pleasure.

She breathed deeply, drawing in the musky maleness that hung in the air like a fine veil, a faint trace of a lemony polish mingling with leather, and paper, and a vaguely familiar smell that must be the aftershave he wore.

The desk was bare, except for a large, old-fashioned leather blotter and a leather box that held pens and pencils. The computer terminal looked out of place on the polished surface, beside the accessories of another age. She slid into his chair, leaned back and sighed.

At least there was no picture of Cynthia on the desk! Or was it in a leather folder that matched the desk set—one he could pick up and take with him when he travelled?

For a moment she wished she'd looked around more carefully on her brief visit to his home. Maybe there she'd have found some clue to the persona of the man who was her boss, some idea of his private life.

Get to work, she ordered her reluctant self, reaching out to switch on the computer, and thinking of the report she must tap into its memory.

She settled back in, but the spark of excitement that had filled her first two months was missing, and duty hours on the phone dragged by with a slowness that devastated her.

Office gossip told her that Peter was in Nepal, preparing to bring back a trekker who had been injured in a rock-fall. The young man had to be stabilised before he could travel, which meant it could be a week or more before they returned.

Each time she lifted the phone, her heart leaped into her mouth, then sank back into her boots when she realised it wasn't him on the other end of the line.

I don't want to speak to him, she continually reminded herself, but the reminders had little effect on the reactions of her body when the phone rang, or on the pain that crawled along her nerves when she heard his name mentioned.

CHAPTER TEN

PUTTING on a bright face at home became increasingly difficult, although Melanie was aware that Barry and Kip barely noticed her existence. Should she find somewhere else to live? Or would she leave Brisbane when she left UniversAid?

Then Mario arrived, blowing back into her life at the end of a day at work like the hot wind she'd experienced in Portugal. The leader of her band of 'no-hopers', he had returned to university to complete his degree soon after she'd departed, and was gaining a reputation in Europe as an innovator in sports medicine.

'I had no time to write,' he explained as they walked beside the river together, catching up on the last eight years that their rare letters had barely touched. 'It came up suddenly, this opportunity to travel to the World University Games in Brisbane.'

He accented both syllables of the last word equally, and the peculiar pronunciation made her smile.

'That is the place the angry doctor took you back to, so long ago,' he continued, 'and from there you travelled to your parents' home. I remembered, you see, Melanie!'

He looked so pleased with his cleverness, she had to laugh, although mention of the 'angry doctor' prodded the bruise she carried in her heart.

'So I say *sim* and come to Brisbane and I telephone

174

to your home and your parents tell me you live here already.'

His brown eyes glowed with pleasure, and his smile of delight at his own cleverness made Melanie stop and hug him, clinging to his wiry frame as she'd clung eight years ago. Then she'd fled from Eduardo's persistence, getting as far as the local square before realising that she was alone in a foreign country, and that her only security was back in a house that held both fear and shame.

'You are happy now that you have grown up?' Mario asked her, his arms still holding her loosely as he looked into her eyes.

'I suppose so!' she said lightly. 'I've got a fantastic job and——'

'And someone to love?'

'Love's not important!' she said, gaily brave as she denied her aching heart. 'Not at the moment, anyway.'

His face grew serious as his eyes scanned her face.

'I think for some people maybe not,' Mario replied, with a very European shrug of his shoulders. 'But for you, Melanie, maybe it is! After all, it was love you went searching for when you became tangled up with Eduardo.'

'Do you know so much about love now, Mario?' she teased, hoping to steer him off a subject she had no wish to pursue.

'I do, Melanie,' he said seriously, steering her off the path by the river and down to the bank, where he pulled her down to sit by the water's edge. 'See!'

He pulled a slim wallet from his pocket and opened it to show a picture of a beautiful, laughing girl.

'This is Juanita,' he said simply, the love glowing in

his dark eyes and almost oozing out of the pores of his skin.

Melanie felt its strength like the radiant heat of a fire, and smiled at her old protector.

'I am thrilled for you!'

He nodded, as if accepting only what was his due.

'In four months, we have our first baby,' he told her proudly, and Melanie's love life—or lack of it—was forgotten as they talked of the future, and the lives of the others who had made up their little band.

They walked slowly on towards the shopping centre, stopping to eat at a small Italian restaurant, then meandering back to the flat, hand in hand, like children who were reluctant to part.

'Where are you staying?' Melanie asked, when they reached the shadows of the trees that sheltered the small block of flats.

'We have rooms in one of the university colleges,' he explained. 'I can get a taxi back to there.'

'I'd drive you, but we had that wine with dinner,' she explained apologetically. 'Anyway, come in and have a cup of coffee before you go.'

Kip and Barry were watching television, but they looked up as the pair came in, and were soon caught up in conversation with Mario asking question after question about Portugal, Spain, and then Europe in general.

'You see,' Kip explained to Melanie as they made another pot of coffee, 'Barry and I have been talking about taking a year off and travelling after we're married. Meeting your friend makes it all sound real and exciting.'

Melanie smiled and nodded. She was tired, and

ready for bed. She'd see Mario again while he was here! Surely their questions would keep.

She rejoined the others with a false smile in place, but Mario, who had looked after her so well once before, was not fooled.

'I am keeping you up!' he protested. 'Even long ago you could not adjust to our late hours in Portugal.'

'If you mean eating dinner at ten o'clock at night, I certainly could not,' she told him.

'I will go,' he said, but the other two begged him to stay.

'We'll drive you back when we've had this cup of coffee,' Barry promised.

'Or you could stay here, if you don't mind sleeping on the couch,' Kip added. 'It's quite comfortable.'

Mario looked enquiringly at Melanie, who nodded, and yawned for the third time in five minutes.

'If you're coming back to dinner tomorrow night,' she told him, 'you could stay the night, drop me at work in the morning, and take my car back to the university. That way you've got transport to get back here.'

Everyone seemed pleased with the arrangements, so she said goodnight and left them talking.

'There was a phone call for you earlier,' Kip remembered to tell her as she ducked from the bathroom to her bedroom a little later. 'Someone from work, but he said it wasn't important.'

It couldn't have been another courier job, or they'd have kept trying to contact me, she decided as she fell wearily into bed. Whatever it was could wait till morning.

* * *

Mario handled her little car well, adapting easily to driving on the 'wrong' side of the road. He pulled into a space outside UniversAid's offices, and slipped out to open the car door for her and walk her up the stairs.

'I will see you tonight!' he said, bending to kiss both her cheeks and then raising her hand to his lips before running lightly back down the steps.

'Very touching!'

The deep voice ground out the words as she came into the shadowy darkness of the foyer. She didn't need to wait for her eyes to adjust to the dimmer light to know who had watched the theatrical farewell.

'So you're back,' she said baldly, although her heart was pounding so loudly he must surely be able to hear it, and her breath fluttered erratically in her lungs like a moth trying to escape from a box.

'Just in time to realise how wrong a supposedly sensible man can be in his judgements.' The words were as cold and hard as stones, and every bit as painful as they hit against her. 'Sheer common sense kept telling me I was wrong, but would I listen?' he added, with such cosmic scorn that she felt like punching him.

The lift door slid open, and she hesitated, unwilling to enter such a confined space with him.

'Scared?' he challenged.

'Why should I be?' She gathered up her courage and stepped inside. Now that he was back, her future would be decided one way or the other, but, whether she wanted the job or not, she was determined to fight for her right to be offered it. And fighting began by not backing down!

She watched his profile surreptitiously as he slid the plate into the control, seeing the faint white lines fanning out beside his eyes, and the deep crease that strain had pressed into his cheek.

I'm sure Cynthia doesn't look after him properly, she thought. Why else would he seem so tired and defeated?

The urge to fight slid away, and in its place was a burning desire to reach out and touch him, to hold him in her arms and knead away his fatigue, her fingers light with love.

'Are you going to appoint me to permanent staff?' she demanded abruptly, horror at her thoughts making the words sound more belligerent than she'd intended.

'I suppose I am,' he replied, staring straight ahead at the lift doors as it slid silently upwards.

'Well, don't sound too delighted about it!' Melanie said sharply. 'You either think I'll be a good employee or you don't.' Weeks of frustration fuelled the rage now sizzling within her.

'Oh, I think you'll be a good employee, Melanie,' he said, turning half towards her so that she could see a smile twisting his lips in a way that hurt her.

'But there's a "but", isn't there? Some reservation, like a hangover, hovering in your mind.'

Her voice had risen and the doors had slid open, but the stab of pain the smile had caused had been the final slosh of petrol on the embers of her anger, which burst forth now like the shower of sparks from a firecracker.

'And it's all based on a prejudgement you made eight years ago, before you even met me. Mario and his friends were bad, you decided, "no-hopers", in fact, and it followed I must be bad as well, to be with them. You didn't wonder why I ran away from the Casels' house. You didn't ask if I had a reason. You simply picked me up with a distasteful look on your proper

English face, as if I were something nasty washed up by the tide, and carted me off, issuing orders every step of the way!'

He must have touched the controls again, she realised, for the lift doors had closed, but her anger was not shut off as easily.

'I asked you when I started if you'd hold my past against me. I didn't want to start the job if it meant you were going to put me off after two months.'

'I've told you you can have the damn job!'

He was slumped against the corner of the lift now, his eyes turned up towards heaven as if exasperated once again by behaviour that could only be labelled childish. But Melanie was beyond rational thought as words she hadn't ever wanted to utter burst from her lips.

'I don't want your damn job,' she fumed. 'I don't want to have to keep coming to work, and seeing you, and knowing you're still judging me all the time. I don't want it any more! I can't handle it any more!'

And then, all passion spent, she began to cry, letting go of all the pent-up emotion in a rain of tears she could not control.

'Don't cry, Melly,' he whispered, his hands moving towards her, then hesitating, held at bay only inches from her shoulders. 'Please don't cry,' he begged again in a strangled undertone.

Then the hands descended and he drew her close, leading her out of the lift and into a room she had never seen before. He leaned back on the desk and drew her hard against his body so that she rested between his legs, and felt the security that only seemed to come from being in his arms.

'Is it too late to ask you about Portugal?' he whispered against her hair, and she shook her head, denying the telling, not the question.

'I'd like to know,' he added in a voice that seemed to hold as many tears as she had shed. 'I need to know,' he amended, pushing her back from him so that he could look down into her face.

His skin was pale, and the lines of tiredness seemed deeper than they had been earlier. His eyes held an expression of such kindness, it made her want to cry again, then they crinkled at the corners and he said with a rueful smile, 'Consider making me listen as a kind of penance for my neglect back then.'

His hands rested lightly on her shoulders, while his knees still held her captive.

Would it help to tell it all? she wondered, then knew that maybe it would.

'It's a tacky little story, in hindsight,' she said bravely, holding his gaze as she tried to read his reaction.

'It can't be any worse than I've imagined,' he muttered, leaning forward to brush an apologetic kiss across her forehead.

With halting words, she repeated the full story for the first time, telling him all the little details that had been kept hidden in her heart, freeing all the bewilderment and humiliation she had felt as she finally exorcised the ghost that was Eduardo.

'And the "no-hopers"?' he asked, when she had finished.

'Found me in the square,' she said, smiling now, as a lightness she hadn't felt for a long time invaded her being. 'They'd decided to take a term off university studies and explore their country. They scooped me up and took me along with them. They looked after me better than they would have their own sister, Peter, and insisted I keep in touch with my parents. It wasn't their fault I got sick!'

'So you kept telling me,' he said, smiling at her again in a way that made her want to fling herself back into his arms. 'I owe you, and them, an apology.'

The hands that rested on her shoulders trembled slightly, as if he too felt the magnetic force pulling them together.

I can't fall back into his arms! she warned herself, then, emboldened by the relaxation in the tension between them, she turned her thoughts back to the conversation and said cheekily, 'Well, you can apologise to one of them. Mario is here with the Portuguese team at the World University Games!'

'I thought I recognised him. Followed you halfway around the world, has he?'

The words had a crispness that told her they were back to playing games.

'As a friend!' she emphasised. 'In fact, I think he might have looked me up to tell me all about his beautiful wife and soon-to-be-born baby.'

'And it upset you, that he's got a wife?'

Had he heard the panic in her voice that the word 'wife' always caused her? It had certainly brought her back down to earth with a thud. Little tête-à-têtes like this, with Peter, were definitely off-limits.

'No, I'm delighted,' she said abruptly. 'Now I'd better get to work before Jan sends out a search party. Where are we, anyway?'

'We're at work, Melly. At the place where, not so many minutes ago, you were telling me you didn't want to be! I'll ring through to Jan and tell her you're with me.'

He half turned to pick up the receiver, but his knees still pressed against her thighs and she lacked the will to move away, because her body was convinced it had come home to rest at last. She heard the murmur of his voice, taking in the musical quality of it rather than the words.

Would Jan wonder what she was doing with Peter? Wonder where they were?

'Now, tell me why you don't want to work here,' he prompted softly when he turned back towards her, his blue eyes shining with a tenderness that made her insides dissolve into a shaking jelly.

She shook her head, caught in a net of emotion from which she could see no escape.

'Could it be something to do with an attraction between us?' he asked, the question jolting her head back so that she stared, speechless, into his clear eyes.

'Did you think I didn't feel it, Melly?' he asked. 'Don't you know it has nearly driven me mad? Do you wonder I don't want you working here, when every time I catch a glimpse of you, or smell you perfume after you've walked from a room, I am so distracted from my work I can't think straight?'

A tiny shudder of joy rang through her as she heard the confession, but it was a joy tempered with sadness. Knowing he was attracted to her was hardly enough to wipe away all the other obstacles.

'At first I thought it must be the tail-end of an over-developed sense of responsibility I'd felt for you for a long time,' he continued, and the seriousness in his voice made her look carefully at him again, but his face told her nothing. 'Then I realised it was more than that when I felt like killing that fellow who was asleep in your bed.'

The quiet vehemence of the statement shocked her, especially when she saw the tendon twitching in his clenched jaw and read the remnants of the anger he had felt.

'Now and then. . .' He paused, then seemed to gather strength. 'Occasionally, I imagined that you might have felt something towards me, but every time. . .'

She held her breath, willing him to continue, to say the words she wanted to hear even if a culmination of their feelings would prove impossible.

'Damn it, Melly,' he muttered, pulling her close against him again as if unable to look into her eyes any longer. 'Wherever I went, I kept tripping over your young men! I knew it could never be, and yet. . .'

'And yet?' she whispered, her lips against the warm skin at the base of his neck, where a pulse beat an erratic tattoo in time with her own over-anxious heart.

'And yet what I felt for you continued to grow, until it consumed every fibre of my being. Does that make you want to laugh?' he asked harshly, his hands biting into her shoulders with such force that they were causing pain. 'It was as if I was following a destiny beyond my control—right from the time I came back to Brisbane like a migrating bird, to the place where I'd first met the jolting loss of not having you by my side, knowing I would probably never see you, and determined not to look for you, but here in case fate ever decreed that it was meant to be!'

Was he saying he'd felt something more than lust for her that night in Portugal? Was he saying that the cold, despairing anger had been his protection against what he saw as an irrational appeal, the forbidden attraction between doctor and patient?

'You thought I was a spoilt, self-indulgent little brat,' she objected, remembering the many times he'd labelled her that way.

'And I tried to make myself believe it,' he assured her, 'however much my instinct told me there was more to you than that.'

The doubt in him embarrassed her, and her eyes dropped to study the patterned carpet on the floor, her mind too confused to argue with him.

'Then I'm sitting in my own office, resigned to a life where work is more important than a permanent relationship, more or less at peace with the world, and you walk into view, your hair so much more golden than I'd remembered, your smile so much more beautiful, your body so infinitely desirable I wanted to reach out and pull you into my arms, to hold you close like this, and feel your heart beating against mine.'

The words had stopped making sense, but some subliminal message held Melanie still.

'Then all the glowing excitement faded from your face, and I knew you didn't want to see me. I felt betrayed. My stupid dream splintered into a thousand fragments and I almost hated you. How could I stand to see you round the office every day, to be reminded of my own stupidity in keeping such a fantasy alive?'

'But you had Cynthia,' Melanie bleated, hoping that speech might bring her back to reality from a dream in which she seemed to float, a dream of love, unmentioned yet, but surely getting closer with every syllable he uttered.

'Cynthia and I agreed to go our seperate ways after I returned to London eight years ago,' he said quietly.

'You didn't tell me! You led me to believe she was here!'

Melanie twisted indignantly out of his grasp, needing to see his face, to try to read what lay behind this extraordinary confession.

'It was a protective reflex, Melly,' he confessed, the strange twisted smile hovering again on his lips.

She waited for more, but there was nothing, just her and Peter, locked in a strangely non-sexual clasp, his face portraying a shadowy reluctance that looked almost like fear.

'Is that all?' she demanded, when the shadows spread across her like a heat-deadening cloud and coldness began to seep into her bones.

'It's enough stupidity for one working morning, surely,' he said, self-mockery back in his strengthening voice, as he pushed her away from him and stood up, looking over her head towards the lift foyer. 'Enough to explain why I was reluctant to have you working here! Travelling with you nearly drove me demented with the effort of keeping my hands off you. Then you went off on your own to Africa, and that was worse, because I couldn't sleep for worrying what might happen to you. Then there was Barry! Can't you understand what seeing you with other men does to me, Melanie Ashcroft, or is all your compassion reserved for your patients?'

'I meant is that all you're going to say about your feelings for me?' she asked in a tight little voice that barely hid the quaking of her heart.

'What else do you want?' he roared, all restraint gone as he flung his hands in mute appeal towards the heavens. 'Blood? I tell you I love you to distraction and you say "is that all"!'

'You didn't actually say you loved me,' she pointed

out, the words fluttering on her breath as she held a growing delight and excitement only barely in check.

'Didn't say I loved you?' he thundered, glaring down at her. 'What else is this whole sordid confession, this great blurting out of an idiocy that has hampered my life for the past eight years?'

He paused for a moment, but it was only to take a breath, because the tirade continued to rain down on her head.

'And how do you think I felt when every time I tried to say it earlier your boyfriend would appear and carry you away from me? I love you, Melly,' he raged in a very unloverlike voice, but the words held the music of the angels to Melanie's ears.

'Then maybe you should kiss me,' she said hopefully, tilting her face up towards him with a prim little smile hovering on her lips.

He groaned and pulled her close again, pressing his lips to hers with such burning hunger that she was shaken by the magnitude of the power she'd unleashed. This was not just a kiss that sealed a love long blooming, but a triumphant taking and giving, a passionate pledge of such fierce possession, her body quivered with the might of it.

As his lips slid away to press against her still bruised temple, she dragged air into her lungs, trying to steady the pounding of her heart, and the tumultuous beating of her pulses.

'I love you, love you, love you, Melly,' he repeated as his lips tracked back towards her mouth, already parted to drink in the taste of him, to capture again the spirit of the conquest they both had made at last.

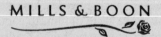

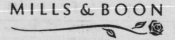

To celebrate 10 years of Temptation we are giving away a host of tempting prizes...

I	F	G	N	I	T	I	C	X	E
A	O	X	O	C	A	I	N	S	S
N	O	I	T	A	T	P	M	E	T
N	B	V	E	N	R	Y	N	X	E
I	R	O	A	M	A	S	N	Y	R
V	C	M	T	I	U	N	N	F	U
E	O	H	U	O	T	M	V	E	T
R	N	X	U	R	E	Y	S	I	N
S	L	S	M	A	N	F	L	Y	E
A	T	O	N	U	T	R	X	L	V
R	U	O	M	U	H	I	A	A	D
Y	W	D	Y	O	F	I	M	K	A

TEMPTATION	ROMANTIC
SEXY	SENSUOUS
FUN	ADVENTURE
EXCITING	HUMOUR
TENTH	ANNIVERSARY

PLEASE TURN OVER FOR ENTRY DETAILS

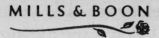

MILLS & BOON

HOW TO ENTER

10⁴ All the words listed overleaf below the wordsearch puzzle, are hidden in the grid. You can find them by reading the letters forward, backwards, up and down, or diagonally. When you find a word, circle it or put a line through it.

Don't forget to fill in your name and address in the space below then put this page in an envelope and post it today (you don't need a stamp). Closing date 31st May 1995.

Temptation Wordsearch,
FREEPOST,
P.O. Box 344,
Croydon,
Surrey
CR9 9EL

COMP395

Are you a Reader Service Subscriber?   Yes ☐ No ☐

Ms/Mrs/Miss/Mr _____

Address _____

_____

_____ Postcode _____